chicks ahoy

D0040588

chicks ahoy

LYNDA SANDOVAL

SIMON PULSE
NEW YORK LONDON TORONTO SYDNEY

This book is a work of fiction. Any references to historical events, real people, or real locales are used fictitiously. Other names, characters, places, and incidents are the product of the author's imagination, and any resemblance to actual events or locales or persons, living or dead, is entirely coincidental.

SIMON PULSE
An imprint of Simon & Schuster Children's Publishing Division
1230 Avenue of the Americas, New York, NY 10020
Text copyright © 2006 by Lynda Sandoval
All rights reserved, including the right of reproduction in whole or in part in any form.
SIMON PULSE and colophon are registered trademarks of Simon & Schuster, Inc.
Designed by Paula Russell Szafranski
The text of this book was set in Berkeley Book.
Manufactured in the United States of America
First Simon Pulse edition June 2006
10 9 8 7 6 5 4 3 2 1
Library of Congress Control Number 2005930051
ISBN 13: 978-0-689-86441-4
ISBN-10: 0-689-86441-8

For Terri Clark—BFF

I couldn't have done it without you!

<SWAK>

Thanks also to

Ann Voss Peterson, Nicole Burnham,
Cathy Jones-Gooding, Isaura Vargas,
Angie Bowman, and of course Barb Thomas.
And a shout-out to the kids at the Cruisemates.com teen bulletin boards for all the help and feedback!

chicks
ahoy

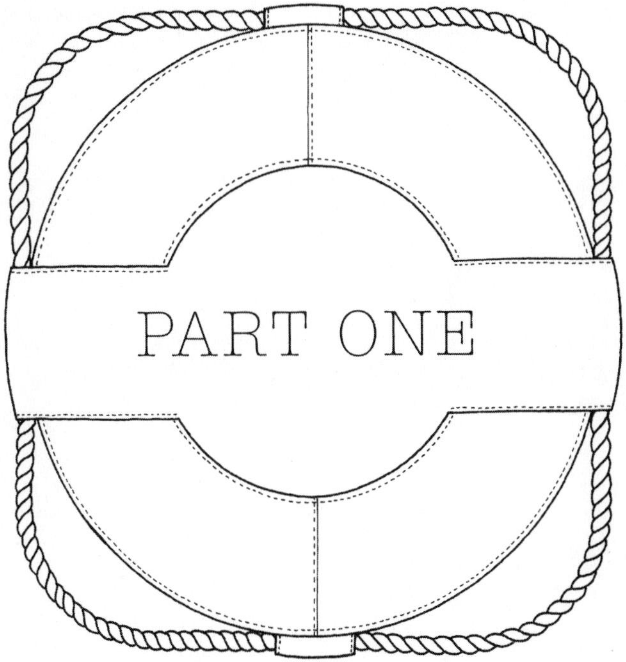

PART ONE

chapter one

How I~~'m Going to Spend~~ My Summer Vacation

^Was Supposed to Spend

by Camille Tafoya

THIS ASSIGNMENT BLOWS. Just FYI.

Not that any teacher in the history of formal education has ever given a rat's ass what we (students) think about THE DUMBEST ESSAY TOPIC EVER CONCOCTED, i.e., this one. ARGH!

How about an essay on Why Guys Totally Suck? I could fill volumes on that one, as could—I'm sure—half the school. More precisely, the FEMALE half. Alas, no. We are forced to fall back on the LAME ol', SAME ol' topics, year after freakin' godawful year.

I mean, come on. "How I'm *Going to* <wink, wink, nudge, nudge> Spend My Summer Vacation"??? Sorry, but . . . does Mr. Wilmington really think this is a clever enough twist on that tired-ass, played-out cliché of a subject that we won't notice his extreme lack of teaching creativity? News flash, Big Guy: not so much.

Can I just mention, while I'm feeling indignant and the rant is fresh, that promoting boredom-induced brain cell death and forcing environmentally conscious students to participate in global deforestation via needless paper wasting—all for the sake of BUSY WORK—is NOT an example of world-class education?!

My summer plans? SHAHHHH, EXACTLY what I want to write about. Yeah, NOT. I don't even want to THINK about them.

Okay. Fine. Wilmington's an adult, and I'm a lowly minor without a vote, so I'm writing. I'M WRITING! (Under duress) However, since I don't actually have to turn in this ridiculous essay-that-is-really-just-a-time-killer-so-Wilmington-can-work-on-his-sci-fi-novel-during-class, what with it being an EXTRA CREDIT assignment I don't NEED two weeks before the end of the school year (—DUH!), I'm going to lay it all on the line. And then, of course, burn every page so no one ever reads it.

How I will *actually* spend the all-important vacation before senior year is totally up in the air, at this point. Instead, let me fill you in on how my best friend, Jiggy Yearling, and I were *supposed to* spend our summer and why the whole plan went straight to hell in a matter of a couple of crappy weeks. Brace yourself, because it's a big, ugly, convoluted tale of woe. The subtitle of my essay is, ironically enough, Why Guys Totally Suck. So, here goes:

The whole fiasco began just before spring break of

junior year, right in the middle of the main "promenade" (hallway, in less pretentious public school terms) of Midwest Academy, which is Jiggy's and my snooty private high school, a place you really have to GET to fully grasp my dilemma. So, here are a few details about the ol' Mausoleum:

MA is comprised of a number of stately redbrick buildings that sit in the middle of a sprawling green campus near Madison, Wisconsin. It boasts proud academic and sports histories, which are photo-chronicled for the world to see, should they so desire, all along the wide promenade of the main building.

Most of the students are filthy rich and perfect and drive nicer cars than either of my parents. The rest of us—mostly the offspring of local academics—huddle in the shadows of this glowing social nucleus, sort of trying to bask in the feeble rays reflecting off their veneered teeth and Tiffany bling-bling.

Though my family doesn't hurt for cash, I am neither filthy rich nor veneered. In short, I would probably fit in much better at the public school, not that the parentals have listened to my reasoning about that. Why would I ever prefer to attend public school after being accepted into the über-prestigious, supercompetitive MA? they wonder. Hork.

Yeah, here's the bottom line. There are exactly THREE reasons I was accepted to the joint in the first place: (1) because my mom is a well-known, well-published archaeologist and a prof at nearby University of Wisconsin (GO

BADGERS!); and (2) because my ultra-personable cruise ship captain dad serves on the city council and knows, basically, everyone. (Not to mention, everyone harbors the misconception that he can get them discounts on cruises. WAKE UP! HE CAN'T!). But mostly (3) because my maternal grandpa, the venerable Virgil Voss, left the school boatloads of cashola in his will.

Number three was the *true* deciding factor, because we're talking BOATLOADS of cash, with a capital B. Like, basically, ALL of it. Why lie?

I mean, sure, it's wicked cool that the science lab at our school is named after my gramps. But along with that distinguished legacy comes a mondo gigungous ball-and-chain of PRESSURE to live up to the family name. Since day one at MA, I've been expected to set an example, which completely cramps my style and totally isn't fair, anyway. Just because Gramps was an exemplary scientist and well-respected philanthropist doesn't mean I inherited any of his positive traits.

Yadda, yadda, I could go on, but I won't. That's my life at MA in a nutshell.

I have always occupied a nondescript but very comfortable position on the "not quite up there, honey, but nice try" B-list of the school's unspoken (but very real) social class strata.

Then . . . along came BRETT.

I HAAAAAAAAATE admitting how stunned and sort of humbled I was when BIG-time popular, looks-like-Johnny-Depp-except-not-old, Brett Mason asked me out that day before spring break, because it makes me sound like I need a self-esteem support group and one of those *Chicken Soup for the Unpopular Dork's Soul* books (and maybe I do). But, I kid you not, this hook up came out of left field, and come on—guys like Brett Mason (veneered) DO NOT ask out girls like me (not even decoupaged), which should've been my first clue.

But, that's the point. I *had* no clue. All I had was LUST. And a lot of flattery-induced tunnel vision.

I can safely say I was penciled in on the A-list for those few short Brett months, even though I was WELL AWARE my temporary list appearance was nothing more than a cool-by-association deal. Still. So, yeah, here's a tip:

Never let a GUY—even a top-shelf, A-list, über-hottie like Brett—keep you from studying for an important test like, ohhhh, the freakin' SAT. The results of thinking with your hormones rather than your BRAIN have far-reaching ramifications, wayyyyyy beyond just having to sit through that excruciating, butt-numbing, eye-glazing, repetitive-stress-injury-causing test more than once.

What? you ask. Repeat the SAT?

Sadly, yes. The ugly and pathetic truth is, I was so consumed by this unexpected, social-boundary-crossing BOYFRIEND of mine that—I'm ashamed to say—my SAT studying slipped into the unimportant category until it was WAY beyond too late. I won't even torture you with my scores. But to say I blew the SAT is . . . well, a gross understatement.

And it's not just the test scores that bit the dust either. My life took some totally unexpected twists and turns during the whole Brett era, spitting me out at the end in a completely different place than I'd ever imagined. It's sort of unbelievable when I lay it all out.

While things were—I stupidly thought—going well between Brett and me, I'd begun plotting my entire pre-senior summer vacation around staying in Madison to spend time with him, which would've taken some serious lobbying on my part. Dad's on the ship every summer, and my mom goes on archaeological digs with grad students during break, so I always fly out to Boulder, Colorado, to stay with Grams Tafoya while they're away. It usually rocks; I've done it since I was a kid. Even better, the last three summers, Jiggy has gone with me, because her parents have weird jobs too (which is what brought us together at the beginning—a whole 'nutha story), and she was set to go with me again this year. But, when I explained my desire to stay near Brett, Jigs was totally up for hanging out in Madison too. She's way go-with-the-flow, which is one of the many reasons I love her to death.

Jiggy and I had big plans . . . chilling on the union terrace listening to live music, playing Frisbee at James Madison Park, boating on Lake Mendota and Lake Monona, FINALLY getting to attend the Rhythm and Booms fireworks show on July Fourth . . . not to mention sneaking into the High Noon Saloon every now and then if we could work the whole fake ID angle.

And Brett. My biggest plan was BRETT.

So, as much as we WANTED to stay with Grams for the summer, we also wanted to stay home. I just didn't know how to break it to anyone, and, more than anything, I didn't want to hurt my grandma's feelings. Turns out, I didn't have to.

Get freakin' this:

Grams shocked the hell out of all of us by ELOPING just after Christmas, and I'm not even kidding. She's, like, seventy-something! It sounds like some ridiculous soap opera story line, but it's TRUE. She hooked up with this rich guy, twenty years her junior, who owns some kind of a dot-com empire that HOPEFULLY doesn't have anything to do with porn (Dad's checking into it). After a whirlwind courtship that pretty much none of us knew about, they road-tripped to Las Vegas and got hitched in a little white, neon-illuminated chapel, just like Britney and what's-his-face—that guy from her hometown—did, pre-Federline. I AM SO NOT KIDDING! Only, Grams's marriage wasn't annulled fifty-five hours later. In fact, I've never seen her happier, and she SO deserves it. My dad met his new step-dad (trippy!) and approves, so none of us are worried about Grandma's welfare like we were when we initially found out.

But the point is, after the elopement, when she told us all that she wanted to go on a lavish six-month, around-the-world trip with Stepgrandpa Lotta Bucks, I was all, "YOU GO, GRAMS!" because it worked perfectly with my secret plans. I could launch my campaign to stay in

Madison, and Grandma didn't even have to know that I hadn't 100 percent wanted to stay with her for the summer.

Perfectamundo.

So, *during* Brett and *pre*-SAT but *after* Grandma got her groove back (you still with me?), Jiggy and I somehow convinced our parents we were responsible and mature enough to be unsupervised for the summer. The facts were, (1) we couldn't go to Grandma's; (2) Jiggy doesn't have grandparents who are still alive, because her parents are older; (3) we're almost eighteen, and total nonproblem children; so (4) it only made sense to allow us to stay in Madison for the three short months before senior year began.

Right?

I mean, Jiggy and I would be *together*—and everyone knows our personalities balance each other out quite well. Her parents are primatologists, and they head off to Tanzania or where-the-hell-ever for three months each year to do fieldwork with the chimps. Plus, neither of us has *ever* complained that our parents have basically gone AWOL for several months a year since we were kids. THAT was the guilt-trip trump card in our Pre-Senior Summer-in-Madison campaign. We both DESERVED this bit of freedom. It was the whole showing-your-parental-trust thing. Paybacks. Whatever.

And we HAD IT locked up.

Riiiiiiiight up until Mom and Dad got a load of my

dismal SAT scores, at which point that whole "summer lovin'" plan went straight out the window.

Bye-bye, fun parent-free summer in Madison. Bye-bye, romantic evenings with Brett. Bye-bye, Rhythm and Booms fireworks show.

So, life sucked enough, right?

Ha. And I thought things couldn't get suckier. . . .

Mere DAYS after the SAT debacle, I found out that Brett only asked me out in the first place because he and his cretinous buddies had a running BET about "how many virgins they could bag" before graduation, if you can believe that. It's SO much like one of those tacky teen sex-and-toilet-humor movies, which are awesome to watch, but you don't want your life to resemble one!

Turns out he never really liked me at all. I was just one more meaningless virgin conquest in a long line of them. UGH. And, while I'm on the topic, HOW EXACTLY DID THEY KNOW I WAS A VIRGIN, ANYWAY?!? Was it just an unfortunate assumption? Was it how I dress? Or walk? Or, worse: Do I exude some sort of LAYDAR that shows everyone how sexually inexperienced I am? *Yeah, dude, how about Camille Tafoya? I guarantee no guy has slipped it to HER.* UGH! The indignity.

The sad and unfair truth is, Brett is HOT. And charming, in that whole Tom-Cruise-in-*Top Gun* kind of way, if you even remember that flick. He really had me snowed, which does NOTHING for my self-esteem. For the record, I DID NOT sleep with him, but—and I admit this with profound regret—I came as close as a person can without actually going all the way. GLUG. (Use your imagination, because I am not committing the details to paper, now or ever.)

Brett—gutless sociopathic ASS that he turned out to be—deemed our little tryst "close enough," added me to his list of bagged virgins, and moved on. AND THEN TOLD EVERYONE. I shit you not. EVERY freakin' ONE.

He might as well have taken out an ad in the paper.

The entire school is now aware that (1) I was pinpointed by a gaggle of horny senior guys as a pathetic virgin in need of bagging; and (2) I was actually naive enough to believe Brett Mason would ever genuinely like me; but worst of all (3) that I gave it up to the dude in a matter of WEEKS.

So, to make a long story . . . well, totally LONG, I quite possibly blew my shot at admission into CU Boulder over this lying, reputation-destroying, morally reprehensible, virgin-bagging creep. I'm still sorta beating myself up over the whole thing. Especially because . . . I really thought I cared about the guy. And yes, I thought it might actually be mutual. Yeah, I know, GULLIBLE. I am fully aware that I raised the bar on DUMBASS behavior.

The only positive aspect to this major BOMB Brett dropped into my world is, I no longer have any reason to stay in Madison for the summer, which is a damn good thing considering my parents have no intention of letting that happen.

But WHERE Jiggy and I will end up is ANYONE'S guess!

FROM: GetNJiggy@midwestacademy.wi.edu
TO: YearlingPhD@gorillas-inc.org
TIME: 4:11:59 p.m., CST
SUBJECT: Just rambling

Hi, Big Bro!!

It's me, Jigs, your WAYYYYYYYYYY littler sister, comin' at you cyber-live from lovely Madison, Wisconsin. How are things in gorilla land? Hope you're single-handedly stopping the evil poachers and doing your utmost to curtail the illegal bushmeat trade in your part of Rwanda. (HOO-RAHH! Go Dr. Yearling! <g>)

Mom and Dad have already left for Tanzania, but you probably already knew that. I'm sure they e-mailed you, even though I haven't exactly heard from them since they got there. I'm sure they're too busy to let me know they got there all right. But, you guys probably talk all the time, right? If so, let them know I'm thinking about them and that they can drop me an e-mail if they want to say hi.

I'm living with the Tafoyas again—remember my best friend, Camille? I don't know if Mom and Dad mentioned that, but I'm sort of assuming they didn't. :-\ Camille and I were supposed to stay here in Madison for the summer alone. That's right, your little sister was supposed to spend three MONTHS completely free of adult supervision! We were going to make a Girls Gone Wild/Pre-Senior Summer video, sleep around with incoming jocks at UW's football camp, and sample every illegal drug on the black market.

I'm JUST KIDDING! Don't get on the horn to Mom and Dad. Not that they'd care. Or NOTICE. Besides, it turns out we're NOT going to stick around in Madison alone, because Camille screwed the pooch BIG-TIME on her SAT, and her parents are freaking out. She has to retake it in the fall so she can get into a decent college, and they think she needs adult supervision to Stay On Task with her studying. (They're probably right, but don't ever tell Camille I said that.)

Anyway, I'm home (at the Tafoyas') alone at the moment, and I'm just sitting here thinking about life. Our lives. And suddenly, a question that has nagged me for years popped into my mind once again. Doesn't it ever strike you as ODD that our parents named us after famous primatologists (or paleontologists, or whatever the frick your namesake was)? I mean, DUDE, they named you Louis Leakey Yearling. YOUR MIDDLE NAME IS LEAKEY, for God's sake! That CAN'T POSSIBLY be a date-getter for a guy.

And then my name—JANE GOODALL Yearling. I don't know how YOU feel about yours, but this bothers me, and it's nothing against Ms. Goodall, who is an awesome, amazing, admirable person. But, HELLO, I'm not her. I'm ME, but as it turns out, that equates to NOBODY. It's like M&D couldn't even see us as unique individuals, with our own identities. They just wanted little clones of their career idols or something. I mean, think about that for a moment. They couldn't turn their attention away from their all-important careers even for a MOMENT to see the unique little babies they created or to choose names that would celebrate that individuality. I have someone ELSE'S name—someone more important to my own parents than I am. CAN YOU IMAGINE HOW THAT MAKES ME FEEL?

It's weird, and if you want to know the truth, it makes me feel invisible. All of you make me feel invisible, as a matter of fact, and ya know what, bro? What the hell? I'm just going to tell you EXACTLY what I've been bottling up for what seems like forever.

You're all so caught up in your Important Life's Work, I feel like I'd have to dress up in a hairy black or brown primate costume to even catch your attention for a MINUTE. One of my teachers is pregnant, and when she told the class that she loved teaching but that the most important job of her life would be raising her children, I committed the socially crippling faux pas of bursting into tears and fleeing the room like some loser!

Did any of you ask me what I would be doing this summer? Mom and Dad didn't even ask me! It's like they just assume I'm going to trundle along doing the right thing, making the smart choices, just like ALWAYS. They can shove me here, or pack me off there, and I'll just go with the flow without a single word of complaint. I'm SEVENTEEN, and they didn't even give me the requisite no drinking-no drugs-no sex lecture before they left. For three MONTHS!

Do they think I'm a Girl Scout or something??

Like, how do any of you know whether or not I'm

sexually active? Or whether or not I drink? Or do drugs? Incidentally, I'm not, unfortunately; I don't—and I don't, but THAT IS BESIDE THE POINT. I could be a big, giant, smack-shooting, pole-smoking slut and none of you would even notice.

I feel like a ghost in my own life, Louis. Mom and Dad just walk through me, and they might feel a little cold chill, but they never stop to investigate where it's coming from.

I'm not sure if you remember, since you were already in college, at that point, but do you know they dressed me up as a damn baby chimp for EVERY SINGLE HALLOWEEN until I was able to pick my own costume? Hell, I swear they'd be happier right this very minute if Mom had given birth to BONZO rather than to me, and let's face it: I was a HUGE oops baby. A career woman like Mom doesn't just VOLUNTARILY get pregnant at forty-six years old. I'm surprised they didn't just get rid of me before I was born. I'm a nobody in this family, and I'm a nobody to you. And it's not FAIR!!!!!!! And I don't CARE if I sound like a tantrum-throwing seventh grader right now! Why do I always have to hold in my feelings?

All I've done my WHOLE life is be obedient, study hard, stay out of trouble. I'm a GOOD KID, and even that doesn't earn me any kudos. What do I have to do to get noticed in this family???? Commit murder? Get knocked up by the art teacher? Boink the whole UW football team? Pass out with alcohol poisoning at a frat party I sneaked into UNDERAGE?

I'm asking you, Louis, because I'm totally bumming about this right now. I've waited and waited and waited my WHOLE life for things to change between me and our parents, and nothing EVER does. I'm almost an adult, and I still feel like the kid no one wanted! I'm an afterthought. Forget branch—I'm not even an ORNAMENT on our family tree. I'm not even the cheesy metal hook for the ornament. I feel like I've missed growing up in a real family.

I'm busting my ass trying to choose a college, but it seems like Mom and Dad aren't even interested because I'm not getting a degree in primatology like you did. It's like the three of you are in this little closed society and I'm on the outside looking in. ALWAYS on the outside. I hate it.

I want real parents.

I want to be lectured and have a curfew. I want Mom to tell me I'm wearing too much makeup, and I want Dad to bark, "No way are you leaving the house in that getup!" when I'm heading out to a house party in some trampy outfit. I want them to sniff my purse to check if I've been smoking, and to give every guy who comes near me the third degree. I've never even been GROUNDED, and it's not because I haven't deserved it—it's just because they don't even NOTICE me enough to discern when I might need to be on house arrest! I want household rules so I can rebel against them, just like every other teenager! IS THAT SO MUCH TO ASK????????

<sigh> Who am I kidding? I'm never going to send this.

Back slooooooowly away from the rant, JIGGY! Let's take this stupid e-mail from the top.

<DELETE>

FROM: GetNJiggy@midwestacademy.wi.edu
TO: YearlingPhD@gorillas-inc.org
TIME: 4:33:37 p.m., CST
SUBJECT: Hello from your little sister

Dear Louis—

Hi, big brother. Hope all is well with you in Rwanda. Everything is fine here, same as usual. School's out after this week. For me, that is. Mom and Dad are already in Tanzania, and I'm living with my best friend, Camille, for the summer, like usual. We normally stay in Colorado with Camille's grandma, but this year we were supposed to stay in Madison. It looks like things might change, though. Long, boring story. I don't know where we'll be for the next three months, but I'll keep you posted.

Well, I guess that's all for now. Be careful of the evil poachers, and write me back when you get a free moment.

Love, Jiggy

P.S. Say hi to Mom and Dad from me if you talk to them.

www.NobodyGetsJiggy.com

Those of you who read my blog regularly have heard this topic before, but hey, it's MY blog and

MY blog rules. For those of you who fell into my blog world for the first time, the rules are:

1. I can blog about whatever I want, as often as I want to, even if I'm obsessing. Therefore—

2. If you don't want to read my blog, feel free to leave.

3. I have been the nice one my whole LIFE. Hence, I don't have to be nice in my own blog universe.

4. The only opinion that counts in my blog universe is mine.

In short, I can whine if I wanna. If you don't agree, well, don't let the cyber-door hit you in the cyber-ass as you leave. Sayonara—get your own damn blog. Still, I'll keep it short this time because I don't have anything new or earth-shattering or insightful. Just the standard rant: Parents Suck Ass. Brothers Suck Ass. Being in a family sucks ass, especially if you're me. This blog entry sucks the most ass of all, so I'm outta here until I have something more intelligent to say about the topic.

Have a suckass day.

Love, The Goddess of NobodyGetsJiggy.com

chapter two

"Hey."

"Hey," Jiggy replied, emitting a distinct lack of enthusiasm and a wicked-strong preoccupation vibe. It didn't take a rocket scientist to realize that she wasn't exactly having a stellar afternoon. The whole aura in the room was draggy, depressed, grayish, which mirrored my own mood perfectly.

I'd gone out for a run to work off stress and clear my mind after the torture SCHOOL has morphed into, ever since I'd been unfairly branded a Betty Crocker Ready-to-Spread Ho-bag. I'd been jogging along, minding my own biz, but no. Brett the Malevolent and his deviant wingmen from Hell drove by honking and hooting and talkin' smack, JUST in time to destroy any endorphins I may have worked up in the two miles I'd suffered through. They've had their boyish fun—now WHY CAN'T THEY JUST LEAVE ME ALONE? On the listless jog home, I realized I didn't care WHERE Jiggy and I had to spend the summer as long as it was far, far away from every possible reminder of that colossal JAG-OFF. Famous last thoughts . . .

Anyway, now that I was safely ensconced in my house, I didn't want to think about Brett anymore (or preferably, ever again!). I would much rather remain in the oh-so-comfy Land o' Denial and focus, instead, on getting to the bottom of Jiggy's foul mood. Showering would have to wait. I stopped short at the end of the bed, yanked my workout tank and jog bra off over my head, then grabbed a clean T-shirt from the folded laundry that had been stacked on top of my dresser for several days now.

I assessed the situation out of the corner of my eye: Jiggy, sitting alone with her laptop, looking like she'd witnessed some evil person drop-kicking a baby seal. It meant one of two things. I went for the lesser of the two evils first.

"Blogging?"

"Done blogging."

I figured. "Let me guess, then. Writing to your brother? Again?" I punched my arms through the sleeves of the well-worn University of Wisconsin T-shirt and pulled it over my head.

She snapped her laptop shut, then rested her back against the headboard. "Writing, wimping out, deleting." She hiked one shoulder and let it drop. "You know the drill."

And, I did. Only too well. Jiggy has this intense love/hate relationship going with her family, which she somehow manages to keep on the down low. She's so sweet and mellow, most people would never even suspect her inner turmoil. Naturally *I* know about it, what with being her best friend and all.

She just has the one brother, Louis, whom I've only met once, but he's nineteen years older than she is and seems more like an uncle than a brother. So it's pretty much like she's an only child. Except, where some parents of only children end up totally micromanaging their kids' lives and turning them into giant spoiled wussies (which of course did NOT happen with me), Jiggy's parents seem to barely even participate in her upbringing.

I don't mean to insult to Dr. and Dr. Yearling by saying that, either. They're really nice, in an elderly sorta way (they are a good twenty years older than my parents). But it's a cold, hard fact. Let me put it this way: Jiggy is the most self-sufficient person I've ever met, because she's HAD to be.

I mean, the rest of us full-on envy Jiggy her freedom. She has her own car, checking account, phone line, cell phone, AND credit card, all of which her parents gave to her so she could take care of her own needs without having to come to them. They NEVER check up on her or give her a curfew or ask where she's going or who she's going with, which sounds like pure, undiluted, chocolate-covered HEAVEN ON EARTH to me. But they also don't show up to our school stuff or read Jiggy's blogs or other writing very often (which may be a good thing, come to think of it). Plus, I've never really seen her dad wrap her in a big ol' bear hug or heard her mom ask if she wants to go to the mall and shop—"just us girls." They're just not THOSE kinds of parents, if you know what I mean.

Jiggy's bitter about it.

She loves her parents and everything, but that jagged resentment is constantly sawing away at her insides, giving her this overall unsettled vibe. And yet, she bottles it all up rather than act out. I've never once seen her be less than respectful of her parents, and think about it: What seventeen-year-old girl is respectful of her family ALL THE TIME? Not yours truly, I can tell you that much. It's whack. There is a trippy distance between Jigs and her parents that makes them seem—and treat each other—like polite strangers.

I totally don't blame her for hating that, but I often wish she could let it go and realize how many people DO care where she's going and who she's going with, or resolve to see her parents' hands-off style as a vote of confidence in her maturity rather than evidence that they never wanted her, and move on.

But who the heck am I to talk?

My parents, God love 'em, drive me nuts a lot of the time too. It's sort of just What Parents Do, although they all have their own unique and annoying methods. But you'd be hard-pressed to convince Jiggy of that. She thinks her mom and dad have cornered the market on parental shortcomings. The closer we've gotten to leaving for college, the worse her obsession has become too. Sooner or later, Jigs is just going to explode. It's TOTALLY inevitable . . . if she doesn't do something about it.

"I have an interesting idea," I said, on that note. I sat on the edge of the bed and tucked one leg under me, then reached out and squeezed Jiggy's big toe. "Why don't you just buck up and send one of the zillion e-mails you write? One click—bing—and it's there. Just like that."

"Because." She blew out this big weighty sigh, and her choppy golden-blond fringe flipped up off her forehead. "My family doesn't really RAGE."

"First time for everything."

"Yeah, but it would open a whole, ugly can of worms, and I don't know if I can deal with that."

"Can you deal with always feeling this way instead?"

She shrugged. "I have for seventeen years."

Good point, but not the best solution. "So, send the e-mail but tell Louis not to say anything to your parents. Invoke the whole sibling-confidentiality rule."

She scrunched her nose. "What if he told them anyway? I know he's my brother, but he's more one of them than one of us. He has GRAY in his hair, for God's sake."

"Well, true. But—" Wait! I knew how to steer her off this mental train track that led straight to depressionville. "Okay, Jigs. What's the worst that could happen if he did tell them?" I waggled my eyebrows at her.

Jiggy groaned. "I don't feel like doing this, Camille." We'd been playing the Worst-Case Scenario game since sixth grade. It always seemed to help us put our worries into perspective.

"I don't care if you feel like it or not. Tell me." I squeezed her big toe again, this time until she yelped and wriggled her foot away.

"Bully." She glared, rubbing her toe.

"WHAT-IS-THE-WORST-THAT-COULD-HAPPEN?" I asked again, overenunciating each word as harshly as I could.

Jiggy's lips twitched at the corners, but she managed to stave off the grudging smile I could see right beneath the surface of her stormy mood. She set her laptop carefully on the nightstand, then sat back and crossed her arms. "Okay. Fine. The worst is that . . . they'd be totally disgusted with me."

I scoffed. Big freakin' whoop. "And what's the worst that could happen if they were?"

"Um . . . well, they could disown me."

I nodded once. Now we were getting somewhere. "The worst that could happen if they did?"

"I wouldn't have any money to support myself."

"So? What's the worst that could happen if you didn't?"

"Hmmm . . ." Jiggy leaned her head back and stared up at the ceiling. She reached one hand up and scratched her nose distractedly. "Unemployment? No, that wouldn't fit since I'm not employed. Duh. Ooh! I know." Her eyes got that rebel glint. "I'd have to become a hooker to support myself."

Yeah, right. Imagining Jiggy as a prostitute was a full-on HAR-DEE-HAR laugh riot. We're talking the epitome of All American Girlism here, what with her long, thick, honey-blond hair, big green eyes, and 4.0 GPA. SO not your traditional streetwalker material—not that I'm exactly dialed in to the prerequisites for that particular line of work. Still. Jigs wasn't even slightly slutty, so hookerish seemed WAY out of the realm of possibilities. But I played along. "What's the worst that could happen with you out there workin' it on the curb?"

Her eyes bugged. "Read the papers, Camille. I could get strangled by some creepy—NO, WAIT!" She bounced forward all excited, then grinned. "Getting choked out would be bad—"

"Uh, YEAH!"

"—but listen. This is even worse, and I know you'll agree. That ass, Brett Mason—"

GLUG!

"—could pick me up for a" —she made quotes with her fingers— "date. And I'd be so desperate for cash, I'd have to do him."

"Oh, my God!" I shrieked, flouncing over onto my back on the bed. That familiar "duped, dissed, and dumped" feeling clenched my gut, but I fought to control it and stay in the much more powerful mode of ridiculing Brett. It wasn't easy. Jiggy was the only person who knew the full-on truth about what had happened between him and me, and she didn't blame me at all. Too bad I couldn't stop beating myself up about it. It wasn't the fact that the entire student body at MA presumed I was having sex. I didn't give a crap about that. Probably more than half the class was having sex—no biggie. What I couldn't purge from my brain was the fact that many of my classmates who used to consider me . . . well, if not cool, at least reasonably decent . . . now viewed me as some sort of pathetic pity screw.

UGH! UGH! UGH!

I wished I could rinse out my brain!

The phone rang one and a half times before Mom or Dad picked it up somewhere in the house. I refocused on the Worst-Case Scenario game and . . . HORK . . . unfortunately, thoughts of the Brett debacle. So much for denial. I sighed, pondering the whole hooker concept again, and then a fresh perspective hit me. "You know? That would actually be a good thing."

"What would? Doing Brett Mason?!"

I rolled my head to the side and frowned. "Not the 'doing him' part. Don't make me puke. Just the part where he propositioned you."

Jiggy pulled a horrified face. "Are you HIGH? A good thing HOW?"

Flat on my back, I still managed to open my arms wide in a big DUH posture. "Because then you could spread it all over the known universe that Brett Mason pays for sex and has a really itty-bitty wanker." I stuck my arm straight up in the air and waggled one pinkie for emphasis.

We both howled with laughter, and Jiggy's bummed-out spell seemed to be broken, thank God. The icky self-recriminations still lurked around the edges of my mind, making me feel like a class-A loser, but I ignored them as best I could.

After we rolled around for a bit, cracking up and making lame SCHLONG jokes, Jiggy stretched out on her side and propped her head up with one hand. "So . . . does he?" she whispered, all conspiratorial-like.

"What?"

She waggled her pinkie back at me.

"Ew, Jiggy, please!" I covered my face for a moment, feeling super hot and nauseated, even though I knew I could tell Jiggy anything and she'd never say a word to another soul. Still. I wasn't exactly used to discussing male genitalia, not even with Jigs. Finally, I pierced her with a fine-I'll-tell-you-but-shut-up-until-I'm-done glare. "It's not like I have a great basis for comparison—A. And, B—I only had the opportunity to see it—"

"Don't you mean 'misfortune'?"

"Huh? Oh, yeah. God, yes. Definitely. I only had the *misfortune* to see . . . IT . . . that once, but I didn't really take a good look." I stuck my tongue out in an "ick" expression.

"Why not?"

"Yuck. I don't know. I didn't want to study the thing, I guess." I flipped my hand. "I mean, you have to admit, that particular body part is not altogether attractive looking. You could make a fair case for its usefulness, but I swear, if I saw something that looked like . . . well, one of THOSE . . . crawling across the floor, odds are I'd scream and hit it with a broom. Any reasonable person would."

Jiggy chuckled. "Doesn't matter, anyway," she said. "I'm just going to assume Brett's is so small that it's barely visible and hardly useful."

I snorted, wanting desperately to think about ANYTHING other than—BLECH—Brett's "weapon of mass reputation destruction," because it made me feel freshly stupid every time.

"Enough about Wanker Junior. Listen," I said, jabbing a finger rudely toward her. "I'm not going to lecture you much, but if you truly want to spill your guts to Louis—and I think you need to—then make like Nike and Just Do It. Who cares what they all think?"

"That's the whole problem . . . I do." She plucked at a thread on the comforter, not meeting my eyes. "It sucks being the odd girl out in your own family. I don't want to make it worse for myself."

"ARGH!" Frustrated with this oft visited but never solved topic, I pushed up off the bed and crossed over to my dressing table. After taking my time to sit, then brushing my perpetually tangled, way too curly hair for a few silent moments, I switched gears, meeting Jiggy's reflection in the mirror. "Jigs?"

She looked over and cocked one eyebrow.

"Where do you think our parents are going to send us this summer?" I grimaced. I know I'd sworn earlier that I didn't care where we went as long as it was far away from Brett, but I did SORT OF care. I definitely wanted to be AWAY, but—sue me—I still wanted to have a fun summer.

She shrugged. "Who knows? They'll probably pawn us off to some other professor."

"Are you serious? Someone here?" Panic seized me.

"Oh." Jiggy frowned. "No, of course not. I mean, the

whole POINT is to get you out of Madison. But, wait—unless they know you and Brett broke up?"

"I sure as hell haven't told them." I could just imagine how THAT conversation would go over. They'd want to know WHY, and then I would have to pass out. CLONK.

"Good. It won't even be an issue then. They want you to STUDY, which they've deemed unlikely if you stay here."

"But then WHERE are we going?"

She tossed her hair and stared up at the ceiling. Her lips twisted in thought. "Maybe we'll end up at some sort of intensive academic camp."

I smacked my brush down, knocking a lip gloss off onto the hardwood floor. "Okay, NIGHTMARE. I don't want to spend my last carefree summer in some stupid camp where everyone is a zillion times smarter than I am."

Jiggy rolled her eyes. "You screwed up ONE test. It's not like you're an imbecile." She was nice enough not to point out the fact that this whole summer's ugly turn of events was my fault, and if we ended up in a brainiac camp, I needed to aim the blame directly at myself, then suck it up and make the best of it, dunce cap or no dunce cap.

Instead, she shook her head. "Really, Camille. As long as we get to spend the summer together, who cares where we go? It'll be fun if we make it fun, and I certainly plan to."

I pondered that, then felt like an ass. She had a point.

"Look. You'll be away from Brett, and that's what you want. Right?"

"Definitely."

"No worries, then. Wherever we end up, we'll make a party out of it. Deal?"

I paused, then sighed. "Deal. I'm sorry."

"It's okay."

I SO sucked as a friend. None of this was her fault. She was being swept along in the riptide of my monumental screwup, and yet she was taking the time to make *me* feel better, like usual. So much so that I felt I needed to revisit the TALK TO LOUIS conversation one more time, so that hopefully she could feel better too. I held up a warning finger. "I'm just going to say one more thing about Louis, and then we'll move on."

"Oh, boy," she muttered, rolling her eyes.

I ignored that. "Getting stuff off your chest is about YOU, not them. You can't carry this around with you all the time."

"I know, I know. I'm trying to get over it, but I don't know. It's not that easy."

"I'm not saying it's easy, but I *do* think it's important. I mean, what do you *want* from your parents? Truly?"

"Truly?" She sat up again, then threaded all her fingers into the front of her long hair. "I just wish . . ." Her words faded off, and she shook her head.

"What?"

"A lot of things. I don't know. That they'd just . . . *notice* me. And give a damn."

"They DO give a damn."

"I guess. At the moment, I suppose, I wish they would've

called to let me know they made it to Camp Chimpanzee unscathed. It's the least—" She stopped, blinked a couple times, then released a startled laugh.

"What's funny about that?"

"Nothing. Literally, not one damn thing. I was just going to say, it's the least they'd expect me to do, after all—call them to check in. But actually, it ISN'T." She grabbed a pillow and hugged it to her chest, her expression all troubled and hollow. "I could take a trip to an unstable war zone and never call and my mom and dad would just putter along, assuming everything was peachy."

"Come on. That's not true," I said, with as much conviction as I could muster. But all exaggerations aside, I sort of got what she was saying. Her parents *did* trust her that much. However, where I saw it as *trusting*, Jiggy saw it as *ignoring*. THAT was the bottom line.

"How about giving them the benefit of the doubt? Maybe they were so swamped getting settled in that they didn't have a spare moment to call."

She tossed me this droll expression. "Right." Her tone was hard and skeptical. "Have your parents ever NOT been able to call you? From anywhere? Under any circumstances?"

I didn't say anything, because the answer was NO.

"My point exactly," she said, flicking her hand with impatience. "Let's just drop it. Talking doesn't do any good, anyway. It's *not* too much to ask to be *noticed* by my family at least once before I'm grown up and on my own."

"No, it isn't," I said softly. "But what can you do?"

"No clue. But I plan to find out. Before college, when it will be too late. Whatever it takes to register on my parents' radar screen, I'm going to damn well do it. In a big way."

Before I could open my mouth to remind Jiggy that the majority of the teenage universe was striving to fly UNDER the parental radar and she should, hence, thank her lucky stars, a knock on the bedroom door jolted our attention away.

"Come in," I called out.

The door creaked open, and my mom leaned her head in. For some reason, it struck me right then that she looked like such a MOM. You know, with the conservative sweater twinsets and her dark hair in the ol' risk-free Suburban bob. Just a touch of lipstick in a "safe" hue. At a moment like this, it was fully impossible to picture her crawling around in the dirt, heading up some historically important archaeological dig. But aside from being MOMISH, she was also a kick-ass scientist. I felt an unexpected rush of pride in her accomplishments and a simultaneous unworthiness to be her daughter. Surely *she'd* never have fallen for Brett Mason's lame-ass mack-throwing and insincere flattery. "Yo, Mama."

She smiled and shook her head at my standard smart-ass greeting. "Girls? Dad and I would like to take you both out to dinner so we can talk about this summer. How soon can you be ready?"

Uh-oh. Jiggy and I stiffened simultaneously. D-day, it appeared, had arrived. "I have to take a shower. Forty-five minutes?" I peeked over at Jiggy again to confirm, and she nodded.

"Wear something nice. We're going to Nadia's."

Double uh-oh. Nadia's is a pricey French restaurant on the corner of State Street and West Gilman. They'd only take us there if they wanted to spring BAD news on us—I was almost sure of it. Academic boot camp, here we come. I decided to test my expensive restaurant = crappy summer theory. "Can I order French onion gratinée *and* dessert?"

"Sure," Mom said. "You can order whatever you'd like."

Triple uh-oh. We were definitely screwed if they were pulling the "whatever you'd like" shtick. Oh well. At least we'd have a great meal before they destroyed our hopes and dreams. What was that old Mary Poppins song? A spoonful of sugar makes the medicine go down?

Wait a minute. I reminded myself of Jiggy's words, my new mantra: We could have fun anywhere, if we chose to.

Even an academic camp.

Even a convent.

Anywhere but here!

. . . Right?

I headed toward the bathroom off my room, turning back toward Jiggy once I was out of my mom's line of vision. I made this horror-flick face and drew one finger across my neck like a dagger. Jiggy didn't say anything, of course, but she sort of narrowed her eyes at me.

Just as I started to close the bathroom door, I heard

Mom say, "And you, young lady, are wanted on the phone."

Curious, I creaked the door open a little wider to eavesdrop for a sec.

"Me?" Jiggy said, unnecessarily, as she maneuvered around all the crap piled around her, then scooted her way off the bed.

"Yep," Mom said, all excited. "Camille's dad is chatting with them now, but it's your parents, all the way from Africa!"

I sucked in a little breath and held it. Jiggy froze for a moment, then, just as quickly, regained her cool. She looked a bit pale and a whole bunch uncertain, though. "Great," she said, in this tissue-paper-thin tone of voice. I knew she was wondering why they didn't talk to her FIRST. That's the kind of stuff she tormented herself with.

As they left the bedroom together, Mom's brown eyes twinkled in this happy-go-lucky way that proved she hadn't overheard a word of the discussion Jiggy and I had just been having. Trust me, there was nothing—zip, zilch, *nada*—happy-go-lucky about Jiggy's relationship with her parents.

chapter three

Before we left for the restaurant, Jiggy had whispered that her parents had given away NOTHING about where she and I might end up for the summer, but had suggested we listen to my mom and dad with open minds. OPEN MINDS?! What the heck did THAT mean? Call us pessimistic—but the whole "open minds" directive couldn't possibly be a good sign. I mean, no one ever told you to keep an OPEN MIND before they handed you a million bucks—see what I'm saying?

I felt a little swirly in the gut region on the drive over, and if the pale cast to Jiggy's skin was any indication, she was just as wigged. Despite my trepidation, I tried to remain excited about indulging in some rockin' French cuisine at Nadia's. It wasn't every day we got to eat here, and I wanted to take full advantage of it.

The restaurant occupies the second floor above the street, and is righteously decked out in white linen, fresh flowers in crystal vases, and flickering candlelight. The aromas of sizzling steak and wine sauce permeated the air, and my appetite soared.

We'd been seated at a primo table by the window, and for the first few minutes we all studied the menus, exclaimed over the yummy descriptions, and ordered our first courses. No one said a word about The Big Topic of Summer, but it lurked in the dining room like an accidental fart everyone was trying to pretend they hadn't noticed.

As I buttered a piece of bread and bit into it, I glanced through the window at the hustle and bustle of downtown and experienced a brief but acute pang of regret that BRETT had ruined my summer in Madison plans.

No more, I ordered silently.

I simply didn't have the stomach for this constant IF ONLYing, and this town clearly wasn't big enough for both Brett and me. So be it.

As if she were psychic, Mom said, "I haven't heard you talk about Brett much lately, Camille." She watched me through the candle glow as she took a ladylike bite of her bread.

ACKKKKKK!!

Jiggy aspirated some water and coughed, while I choked on a mouthful of chewy bread crust. I managed to gag the hunk down, but doing so launched me into a tear-inducing coughing fit.

Holy, holy, holy crap. TOTALLY hadn't expected that.

The absolute LAST thing I wanted to discuss with my parents was my ill-fated hookup with Barbaric Brett. I mean, what if the sex part came up somehow? Let's face it: If Brett's entire posse had been able to discern my virgin status from afar, who's to say my parents wouldn't be able to detect the stuff Brett and I *had* done, just based on my answer? Or my aura? AUGH!!!

I thought I might hurl right there. Jiggy hammered on my back with her fist while I fought to regain my composure and figure out what in the hell to say.

"They broke up, Dr. Tafoya," Jiggy told my mom, saving me the trouble.

I wiped my eyes with the linen napkin, leaving a smear of plum eyeshadow on it, then picked up my water and drank.

"They did?" Mom and Dad exchanged a confused look, then peered over at me.

I nodded over the rim of my water glass.

"Honey, when? Why didn't you say anything to us?"

"She probably just didn't want to talk about it," Jiggy said. "You know how it is."

"That's right," I half-croaked and half-belched—a real date-getter in any setting. After hacking against my hand a couple times, I added, "He's a jerk. Good riddance."

"My goodness." Mom laid a hand near her throat. "I thought you really liked him. He seemed like such a nice young man."

UGH, that SO infuriated me. Was she not hearing the

vehemence in my tone? Had she not just witnessed my near death by bread asphyxiation? WHY WERE MY PARENTS SO OBTUSE?? "Trust me, 'nice young man' is probably the least fitting description of Brett"—I lowered my voice and glanced furtively around, in case someone was around who knew him "—Mason you could possibly drum up. He's an asshole—"

"Camille!" Mom exclaimed, just as Dad said, "Hey, now."

I don't usually swear in front of my parents.

"I'm sorry, but he *is*." I scrunched my napkin in a death grip on my lap. "I despise him—end of story. If I never see his face again, it will be too soon."

Mom's eyes widened, and she blinked over at Dad again before reaching across the table and covering my hand with hers. "Breakups happen to everyone, honey, and I'm sorry you're hurting. But where's this aggression coming from?"

From the murky depths of my violated soul, I wanted to yell at her. Instead, I said nothing.

She tilted her chin down in that gentle maternal reprimand position. "Saying you despise someone is a little over-the-top."

If she only knew.

Dad, on the other hand, has always been more perceptive than the average male, and his senses seemed to perk. "Wait just a minute, here. What happened?" he asked, in this do-I-have-to-kick-some-punk's-ass? tone of voice. You gotta love that about my dad. Still, this conversation was hitting too close to the uncomfortable zone, so I couldn't fully appreciate his willingness to pound in some guy's face on my behalf.

"Nothing," I wailed, unable to hold back the plaintive tone in my voice. "We just . . ." *UGH!!!!!!* "It didn't work out, okay? He's not my type, and I should've known that but I didn't. Well, I did, but I was stupid and went out with him, anyway. It's no big deal. Lesson learned. And I do despise him, Mom," I added, with a reproachful edge. I extricated my hand from her grasp. "I'm SO not being over-the-top by saying that."

"She's not," Jiggy added, in a calm, rational tone. "He's pretty much a jerk of the first order."

"Well, wow. Okay. He sure seemed polite enough. It's just such a surprise."

I scoffed. "Yeah, tell me about it."

Mom and Dad exchanged yet another worried glance, then Dad drilled me with his X-ray father vision. "As long as you're certain nothing happened that your mother and I need to know about, *M'ija*. You know you can tell us . . . anything."

I pushed away my bread plate and squirmed with mortification under my dad's scrutiny. I vied for a calm, controlled tone. "Dad, I swear to you, nothing happened." Nothing I'd share with my parents in this lifetime, thank you very much! I pasted a brittle slash of a smile of my face and went on. "The good news is, you don't have to worry about anything happening in the future, either, because I'm never dating again."

Jiggy smacked my thigh with her hand under the table.

I shot her a scowl. "What? I'm not. I have absolutely no interest in Brett part *deux*."

"Sure, you do. Want to date, I mean. Not all guys are like Brett," she said.

"Yeah, right." I mean, how could you ever be certain? Even Brett had seemed nice and sincere at the beginning. Obviously, I lacked the skills to gauge scum potential in males, so my only alternative was to avoid all of them. "I just want to pass the stupid SAT and get the heck out of Madison for good. Guys totally suck. No offense, Dad." He tilted his head in this way that told me he sort of saw my point, which, strangely, didn't make me feel better.

"Well . . . it's good you want to study," Mom said, but she sounded hesitant. "Don't get me wrong about that. But I'm not so sure about the moratorium on dating. You're a young girl, and there will be a lot of dates—"

Like hell, I thought.

"—and you know what they say: Sometimes the best thing to do after falling off a horse is to get right back in the saddle."

Jiggy cleared her throat behind her hand, and I knew she was thinking, NICE choice of metaphors, Dr. Tafoya. Trust me, the LAST thing I needed to do was ride the ol' pony, so to speak, with some other slimy-ass Brett clone masquerading as a "nice guy" or a "great catch."

This icky conversation was on the verge of completely obliterating my desire for coq au vin. Unacceptable. I knew of only one way to steer my parents away from the fully vomitous topic of Brett. In order to spin this thing, I needed to walk up to the edge and confront the abyss yawning dangerously in front of me.

I squared my shoulders and took a fortifying breath. "Dad, please trust me when I say that the only thing you and Mom need to know about Brett 'the scum' Mason is that I have utterly no interest in him and, even better, I no longer have any interest in sticking around this cow-town for the summer, thanks to him. SO . . . on that note"—I raised my eyebrows at Jiggy for support, and she nodded—"why don't we just get on with what we came here to discuss, so we can all, hopefully, enjoy the rest of this yummy dinner."

I looked from Dad to Mom, then back at Dad again. With more coolness than I felt inside, I interlocked my fingers and rested my forearms on the edge of the table. A moment of silence ensued, and I held my breath.

"Well, we were going to wait until after dinner. . . ."

"We're ready now," Jiggy assured them.

"Totally," I added, in a rushed exhalation.

"Okay, then." Mom and Dad gave us these huge, excited smiles. "Where you're going for the summer . . . ," Dad said, "is up to you girls."

I double-blinked. "Huh?" He never really explained stuff very well, poor guy.

Mom nodded, and Dad continued. "We know you both want to enjoy your last high school summer despite the studying you'll have to do, Camille—"

"Yeah, yeah, I know."

"—so we've come up with some alternatives." They grinned at each other. "And we think you're going to be very excited by the choices!"

"Excited? They thought we'd be excited?" I asked Jiggy, about an hour later as we scuffed along the quickly darkening sidewalk toward home. "And to think I didn't even know that my parents smoked crack."

Jiggy snickered. "Well, you did say you wanted to be away from Brett."

"I know, but I didn't exactly mean on a different *continent*." I flapped my arms in defeat. "Although, the farther away, the better. I guess."

I had to give Mom and Dad props. After dropping the three choices on us, they were at least cool enough to let Jiggy and me walk from the restaurant back to our house in Nakoma so we could discuss everything without them hovering. The walk isn't exactly short—three miles or so—but we needed the time and space to recover from the shell shock, because whatever we chose, we were leaving in about a week and a half.

The thing is, I'd had no idea that when Mom and Dad said I needed parental supervision over the summer, they weren't using the term *loosely*. I had foolishly believed that phrase translated to the more generic ADULT supervision, i.e., someone to crack the ol' whip if I wasn't studying hard enough. Not so much. Apparently after discussing the situation at length with Dr. and Dr. Yearling this afternoon, the four of them came up with the three sort of unbelievable options, which they'd all agreed were best:

Evil Choice Number One: We could head off to Tanzania and live with Jiggy's parents and the other primatologists in the field. Pros? Jiggy's parents, as we all know, are totally caught up in their own thing, to put it nicely, so there wouldn't be a lot of annoying hands-on parenting. Cons? The freedom would be of utterly no use to us, because there was nowhere to go for unsupervised fun. Also, no convenient e-mail or hairdryers or decent coffee (probably), and undoubtedly a battery of painful immunizations before we could even step on the plane. Plus, SAT studying might be rough with limited computer time. Oh, and let's not forget MALARIA. Yeah, NOT.

Evil Choice Number Two: We could fly out with Mom to Argentina and live in tents with her and the undeodorized grad students (not to mention the multitude of really creepy spiders and snakes and rats)—and HELP them on the dig. Ix-nay on the ats-ray, thankyouverymuch. Plus, I didn't want to spend my summer days kneeling in some dirt hole brushing off indiscernible clay pot shards with a nasty little toothbrush, all the while acting like I'd unearthed the Hope freakin' diamond. I knew Jiggy shared my sentiments without even having to ask her, because she's wholeheartedly snake phobic. Let's be honest here, Argentina was out before it was ever in.

Tolerable-but-Unfortunately-Still-Not-Definite Choice Number Three: Dad said he still had some red tape to cut through, but

IF he got everything worked out, we could ship out with him and work on the ol' Polynesian Party Barge for the summer. Key word in that suggestion: WORK. Six whole days a week for, like, a million hours a day, from everything I've heard about cruise ship jobs over the years.

I know, I know, our generation has a stunted work ethic and no goals, blah blah BLAH—think what you will. This was our FINAL summer as carefree high school students, and we only had one shot at making it fun. Call us hedonistic, self-centered, and indulged, but we'd been hoping to take FULL advantage of it, not work ourselves to the bone. That's why it's called summer VACATION. HELLO!!!

Still . . . in the whole scheme of "three options that pretty much blow," the ship would at least have Internet access, television, hairdryers, excellent coffee, social opportunities, a movie theater, ice rink, bowling alley, rock-climbing wall (YAY!), tons of good restaurants, AND . . . plentiful hotties (a fact about which, in my post-Brett, guy-hating funk, I didn't give a rat's ass. But, hey, Jiggy was stoked). I mean, my dad's ship is REALLY sweet—at least for the passengers.

So there were our choices. (1) malaria, (2) rats and snakes, or (3) a more-than-full-time job on an, admittedly, excellent ship.

You do the math.

The choice, if not perfect, was obvious.

A wave of missing Grandma hit me, and I regretted ever thinking I might not want to stay with her this summer.

How I'd give anything to be in Boulder this summer, chillin' on the Pearl Street Mall and taking daylong picnic hikes in Chautauqua Park.

SIGH!

Jiggy and I had walked all the way down State Street, through Library Mall, and had turned onto Park Street along the bottom edge of Bascom Hill, before either of us uttered another word. I finally broke our stunned silence by blowing out a noisy breath. "So, wow. The mystery is over."

"Yeah." She stuffed her hands in her pockets and sort of nudged me with her shoulder. "I hope you're thinking ship."

"I can't believe you even have to wonder." I kicked a rock and watched it skitter ahead on the dark sidewalk. "It wasn't even a contest. But I wish I could be more excited. The ship's not even a certainty yet—not to mention we'll be working, not chilling."

She was quiet for a moment. "Yeah, I wonder what the holdup is? I'd hate to think we might end up in Tanzania or Argentina by default. I never imagined for one second that they'd send us there."

"Ew." I flapped my hands like her mere words had burned me. "Let's not send THAT vibe out to the universe. My dad will be able to get us on the ship. He HAS to."

"I hope so. If you want to know the truth, a whole summer cruising the high seas sounds totally thrilling to me." Jiggy reached up and snapped an oak leaf off of a low-hanging branch.

I crinkled my nose. "Even though we have to work?"

"How bad can it be? I mean, shoot, it's a cruise ship. I can think of a whole lot of crappier places to work. Do the words 'Would you like fries with that?' mean anything to you?"

"You're right, of course." My tummy did this little swirling thing that was part nerves and part excitement. But I had to squelch Jiggy's misconceptions immediately. "I mean, the ship has all kinds of totally cool amenities, like teen nightclubs, a sports deck, and an Internet café, but you know what sucks about that?"

"Um . . . nothing?" she said, in her Captain Sarcasmatron voice.

"Wrong-o." I skipped up ahead, then spun to face her. We both stopped, and I spread my arms wide. "What sucks is that we won't be able to use any of those things!"

A line of confusion bisected Jiggy's brows. "Huh?"

Clearly, she didn't grasp the full suck-value of the ship option. "Jigs, it's not like we're going on an extended vacation. As far as I know, cruise line employees aren't even allowed to use the passenger areas. When we're not working, we have to stay belowdecks."

"Ohhhhh," she said, finally getting a clue. "Are you serious?"

"Dead."

"Wow. That . . . sucks." Her expression dropped, but not for long. "But, I mean, what kind of stuff do they have down below? It's not like a slave ship, right?"

We resumed walking. "Well, no. They have a pool and

gym and movie theater. I think a bowling alley, too. But don't get too pumped—it's totally no-frills." I aimed my thumb upward. "All the really fun and luxurious stuff you associate with a cruise is topside, and strictly for the paying passengers." I shoved my fingers through my hair and started to fret. "But it doesn't even matter, because I'm not sure we'll have all that much free time to hang out even belowdecks." I pondered that. "How do they expect me to study if I'm working my fingers to the bone?" Sure, I'd be away from Brett, but crap. Is this what people meant when they said "Be careful what you wish for"?

Jiggy shrugged nonchalantly, but she looked a little scared by all the bad news I'd heaped upon her. "We'll make a lot of money, at least."

I pondered the kickin' wardrobe I'd be able to buy for next school year and I allowed myself a glimmer of hope. "But what about having fun?"

"I guess I won't be able to keep up with my blog over the summer," she murmured.

We fell silent for a minute, lost in our own bleak thoughts. "I'm really sorry, Jiggy."

She grabbed my hand and squeezed. "Don't apologize. I'm not bumming, I'm just brainstorming."

"Even about the blog?"

She shrugged. "I can always keep a blog journal and do a giant update in the fall. I meant it when I said I don't care where we go as long as we're together. I also meant it when I said I'm excited about the ship, even if is isn't going to be exactly how I expected."

"Really?" I bit my bottom lip.

She nodded. "Let's do our best to look forward to the summer. I mean, think of all the hot guys we'll meet."

NOT. I made a gagging noise. Hot guys + Camille = total humiliation. How quickly they forget. "Uh, is that supposed to persuade me?" I asked.

"Oh, come on. Surely once we're there you'll change your mind about avoiding guys. We'll have so much fun," Jiggy said, reaching out to tickle my cheek with the leaf she'd picked before tossing it on the ground.

"That kind of fun I have no interest in, Jiggy. Please. You, of all people, should know that."

"Look," Jiggy said, clearly unwilling to argue about it right then. "Straight up: Work or no work, guys or no guys, it's still a million times better than Argentina or Tanzania, and *that*, you have to admit."

"Agreed."

"You'll be far, far away from Wanker Junior. And I absolutely won't complain about being in the South Pacific for three straight months."

I smiled, calmer by the moment. Jiggy was right, and I didn't want to compound my misery by copping a shittitude. Dad's ship was a great escape. No one there would even know what I'd gone through at home. I could totally reinvent myself, retrain myself to trust my instincts again. If I worked really hard, I could get my mojo back, AND study enough to rock the SAT in September. I could reclaim everything Brett and his bastard betting buddies stole from me.

"Promise me one thing," I said.

"What?"

"Instead of focusing on your parents for the summer, try to forget them. For three months, just let it go and have fun."

She crossed her arms. "You do know I could say the same sort of thing to you, right?"

"But you won't. My trauma is too fresh."

"You're right, I won't. Yet." She stuck out her hand. "And about my parents . . . deal. I'll just have fun."

"You mean it?"

She gave me a DUH look, then waggled her hand at me impatiently. I shook it. Man, I felt great all of a sudden.

"Good, then," I said to Jiggy. "It's settled. Let's head home and tell my parents we're ready to ship out and make the best of it."

Jiggy cupped her hands around her mouth like a megaphone. "CHICKS AHOY!" she bellowed. If nothing else, this summer would be an adventure worthy of a stupid essay assignment!

www.NobodyGetsJiggy.com

Folks, I am spending the entire summer ON A CRUISE SHIP IN THE SOUTH PACIFIC. Can you believe it? I'm going to take full advantage of my time in the tropics, too. My plans?

1. Get a killer tan (and by killer, I don't mean a melanoma-type killer, just a nice, even, sexy bronze).

2. Get in touch with my inner party girl (who might possibly be on the trampy side, which frankly is okay with me. What happens on a cruise, stays on a cruise. <--- I just made that up.).

3. Break C out of her guy-hating funk, which might be an impossible task. Still, I'm going to try.

4. Snorkel and learn to surf, and finally:

5. FORGET THE FACT THAT PARENTS SUCK, which is the topic of a whole different blog . . . but I digress. I will be focusing on ME for the summer and not on the parentals. So, hopefully, this is the last you'll hear about them until next fall. From here on out, it's all ME ME ME. And FUN FUN FUN. I may not be able to blog from the ship, but either way, I'll catch you all up when I can.

Short and sweet, but I need to shop for bikinis, so smell ya later—

The Goddess of NobodyGetsJiggy.com

chapter four

Ten days later, the school year from hell had FINALLY come to a much-needed end, and Jiggy and I found ourselves caught up in what felt like a giant, fast-paced pinball game in which WE were the balls. I swear, someone dropped a token in the machine called Our Lives, and suddenly we were:

Out of school
Frantically packing
Winging down the highway in a door-to-concourse shuttle
Getting felt up by airport security
Boarding a plane
Exiting the plane, cramped and jetlagged
Piled into a private car sent by the cruise line
Checking into a huge Waikiki hotel

Sitting, near comatose, on the beach for our first sunset
Dead to the world pillow-drooling in the hotel beds
Hurling our tagged luggage into the hallway for pickup
Stuffed in another car from the cruise line

BING! DING! DOUBLE POINTS!—just like that.

Finally, it was GAME OVER, and Jiggy and I found ourselves crossing the gangway from the embarkation point and onto my dad's über-cool ship in Honolulu Harbor. In fact, we were on the way to meet my dad, who'd arrived about five days earlier to do, like, pre-cruise captainy stuff, whatever that included. The ship had just been "repositioned" from a year running Alaskan cruises, so it wouldn't leave for its first Hawaiian cruise until tomorrow evening.

The temperature hovered at a comfortable, beach-breezy eighty-five degrees, and the ocean was this fantastic blue-green color that just begged you to jump right into it. The ship rose up from the lapping waves like a gleaming, white mirage, beckoning us forth into its fantasy world.

The reality of this summer finally hit me.

Wow. I mean, wow!

It's not like I'd never been on a cruise before, but still. This time I'd be with my best friend! Well, we wouldn't actually be *on* a cruise, but you get my drift.

I must say, the best part of this walking-onto-the-ship moment was enjoying Jiggy's excitement as awe and she gaped and squealed at each cool new thing she came across. (And she thought EVERYTHING was cool, which, in and of itself, was cool.)

The worst part was our total uncertainty.

Yep, you heard me. UNCERTAINTY.

Despite evidence to the contrary—i.e., we were HERE and boarding the ship—we STILL hadn't received word from my dad that our summer aboard the S.S. *Ocean Whimsy* had even been approved.

I'm totally not kidding!

We'd flown to Hawaii on the wings of pure hope and desperation, because if this gig didn't work out, our next flight would be straight to the stinky tents of the Argentina dig.

GAK!

God forbid!

Dad (and we) had really hoped for a definitive answer about our onboard employment prior to his departure date from Madison, but no such luck. I mean, he split just a few days after the fateful dinner at Nadia's. What did we expect—miracles? After that, we really hoped for a solid answer at least before OUR scheduled departure date. Again, S.O.L.

Every time I'd spoken to Dad on the phone since he'd arrived in Hawaii, he'd hedged about it. It was all "I'm waiting for a signature from this dude" or, "We have a meeting with such-and-such a panel to discuss things" or, "Don't-worry-just-relax-leave-everything-to-me-and-concentrate-on-enjoying-the-end-of-the-school-year-blah-blah," WHATEVER.

As if that were a remote possibility.

We'd be the *first* to know, he always said. The waiting was *totally* stressful. Frankly, I would've been happier just knowing exactly what the damn holdup was, but Dad didn't choose to give us a moment-by-moment rundown, and, besides, explaining things in a logical way had never really been Dad's forte, I must say. My mom calls him Mr. Non Sequitur.

I suppose we could've taken it as a good sign that our parents (1) had gone ahead and paid for our plane tickets to the Aloha state; and (2) hadn't yet subjected us to any of the immunizations required for overseas travel of the Argentinean or African kind, but we're both worst-case-scenario thinkers (remember?). We wouldn't rest easy until we heard the words "NO MALARIA, RATS, OR SNAKES FOR YOU! Welcome to the ship!"

And, that's it. I swear. That's ALL we expected.

We never imagined the results of all my dad's mysterious planning and meetings and signatures and red tape could end up even better than that. . . .

So, anyway, at the embarkation point, our driver handed our luggage over to some cruise guy, and then my dad's way-cool, way-gay, way-fashionista, way-British, longtime assistant, Maurice, met us on the ship side of the gangway. The three of us did the hello/hug-hug/air-kiss thing, then bustled through the skinny little hallway (he called it a companionway, which was ironic considering you could barely even walk through it side-by-side *with* a companion), and boarded a glass elevator that looked out over the BEAUTIFUL eight-deck central atrium. It featured all that over-the-top color and lighting and decor that you associate with Las Vegas, or something. Maurice yammered the whole time, mostly just small talk and fun ship gossip that kept us laughing.

We got out on an upper deck and followed Maurice into this private area near the bridge called the wardroom, which is where my dad and the other officers go to be away from the passengers and crew and basically cut loose. You know . . . act like GUYS instead of officers: watch sports, drink beer, belch, scratch their manly parts. (Ick.)

Presently, Jiggy, my dad, and I were the only ones there. We sat around a little tile mosaic table adjacent to a porthole window and sipped mango smoothies. Well, Jiggy and I sipped them. My dad went for a cuppa joe. He's not really the smoothie-sipping sort.

"I have good news and bad news," he told us, after we'd gotten past all the requisite how-was-your-flight? crapola. "Which do you want first?"

"The good news," Jiggy and I said in stereo. Really, we'd had enough bad news to last us a long, long time. Maybe he could spring the good news and then just ignore the rest. Yeah! Great plan! Besides, we were anxious to leave the wardroom and explore the ship.

He smiled. "Well, I know how disappointed you girls were that you couldn't spend the summer in Boulder with your *abuela*."

Jiggy chanced a baffled glance my way, which I caught out of the corner of my eye. "Um . . . yeah?" Typical dadspeak.

What did Grandma have to do with our summer on the ship?

He looked smug with his secret. "It just so happens that she and . . . Randolph have a stop on the Big Island the same time the *Whimsy* will be docked there."

I let his words sink in, and once they had, my skin started to tingle. I shrieked, "What? When?" This was HUGE! I glanced at Jiggy, who was clapping. Seeing Grandma, even for a short while, would lend some normalcy to this whack-job of a summer. I know she was from a completely different generation and all, but I could share worries and wishes and weird stuff with Grandma that I'd NEVER share with my parents. She never judged me or made light of my problems. And she always had such good advice . . . the kind that never seemed like advice until I thought about it later, and by then I was beyond that whole not-wanting-advice-from-out-of-touch-adults-who-just-don't-GET-me attitude, and what Grandma'd said usually made total sense. Plus, nothing shocked her. I was tempted to tell her about the Brett fiasco, minus any of the scantily clad details. "Do I get to see her?"

"In July, to answer your first question. And, if all goes well, you two will be able to spend the day with her."

A whole DAY? My heart fluttered more from the words he hadn't said than those he had. I leaned forward a bit. "So I take it that means we got the green light to work on the ship?"

Dad's face changed completely. He looked like he was expecting a fight. "Well . . . that's where the bad news comes in."

Crap! It felt like he'd dropped anchor to the bottom of my stomach. I swallowed hard. I couldn't take the tension anymore. I reached over and squeezed Jiggy's hand in a death grip, waiting for the worst.

Dad pressed his lips together in this sympathetic paternal look and expelled a long breath. "Unfortunately, despite my best efforts, I wasn't able to secure you girls jobs on the ship."

Silence.

Huh? I TOTALLY didn't get it. I mean, why the frig were we here? The blood seemed to rush from my head, leaving me dizzy and dumbfounded.

"B-but—" Jiggy said, finally.

"I know you're disappointed." The skin around Dad's eyes creased with sympathy. "I'm sorry. It's competitive, and there are so many rules about who can and can't work. However—"

"What about Grandma, then?" I asked, in a snitty, pouty, middle school tone I just couldn't control. Unshed tears stung my eyes, and I blinked to keep them in. "If we're stuck in Ratville, Argentina, what does it matter if they'll be here in July? I wish you hadn't even told us. This totally sucks the big—"

"Wait, now. *Calmaté*." He held up a palm. "Let me finish before you start plotting ways to push me overboard. I guess I did explain things a little backward. . . ."

News flash, Pops. You haven't explained jack. I slumped back in my chair and crossed my arms.

Dad sipped his coffee, watching us sulk over the rim of

his mug. With annoying calm, he set the mug down. "The sticking point, just in case you're wondering, was your ages. I couldn't convince them to lower their age requirement from eighteen to seventeen, but—"

"I'll be eighteen in September, though."

"And me, in October," Jiggy added. "What's a few months?"

Dad smiled and sort of shook his head at us. "I know, girls. I know. But rules are rules. Listen. Please. We've come up with a workable alternative, which took a lot of finagling, so I hope you'll appreciate the effort." He paused, as though waiting for our gratitude.

I couldn't dole it out without knowing our fate, so I rolled my hand in the universal "get on with it" gesture.

Dad cleared his throat. "Okay. Well. We've created a special program in conjunction with the career mentoring division of continuing ed at Island-Pacific College. It just received final approval this morning." He paused.

"So?" I said, in a less than fully respectful tone.

"*So*," Dad mimicked, seemingly unaffected by my crabbiness, "you two will be in a work-shadowing situation instead of actually employed by the cruise line. Semantics, really."

Semantics? Shadowing? College? Huh? "Which means? In simple sentences and clear English? Seriously, Dad, just tell us *everything*, good and bad, preferably in chronological order. You're KILLING me. Will we or won't we be working on the ship?"

"Well . . . yes."

"But?"

He grimaced slightly. "But you won't get paid."

Our mouths dropped. We had to work for free? So much for a hot new wardrobe come fall. This really WAS a slave ship after all. Weren't there some sort of maritime child labor laws? I held up my palm. "Please tell me that's the worst news."

"It is. However"—he raised a finger before we could launch into the barrage of protests—"there are a lot of positives to outweigh the no-pay issue, believe me."

"Like what?" I said, feeling über-skeptical and verging on belligerence.

"You will be on the ship free for the entire summer—"

"Which we would've been, anyway, right? You don't generally charge the crew for the privilege of working sixteen-hour days, I assume." I cocked one eyebrow at him to let him know we couldn't be snowed.

"Well . . . true. Then, how about this: You two are sharing a pretty posh stateroom on an upper deck near mine rather than living down in the bilge with the others. Since you're underage."

My snarkiness slipped a bit. Okay, the room thing was kind of cool. I'd heard the crew quarters were kind of like living in a prison cell, except without the luxury of a private metal toilet bolted to the floor.

"And here's what will make this all worthwhile. Trust me." He grinned. "You two lucky girls are free to use all the facilities on the ship."

WHOA. I was still ruminating about the posh stateroom and almost missed that. I mentally pushed the rewind button. Had I heard him correctly? I mean, I'd spent the past week or so programming Jiggy to just FORGET the fun cruise ship stuff she'd heard about because it would all be off-limits to crew. My heart began to pound. I held up a finger. "What exactly do you mean by 'free to use'?"

"Just that. You can use all the facilities."

Blink. Double-blink. "L-like a passenger?"

"You bet."

I heard Jiggy squealing next to me, and my jaw dropped. I never looked away from my dad. "Oh. My. God. You can't be serious."

He somehow misunderstood my deadpanned exclamation for dismay (another clear example of father-daughter/ Mars-Venus communication problems). "Camille, I promise you. I tried everything I could to work out the pay situation and couldn't. This was the best I could do."

Was he high? Who cared! This was the best news EVER. Never one to embrace optimism full-on, however, I felt like I needed concrete verbal confirmation that his words meant what I thought they meant before I could advance to pure celebration mode. I flicked my hand. "Just so there are no misunderstandings"—I repositioned myself on the edge of my seat, then flipped up my index finger—"what you're saying is, we're basically going on a cruise for the next three months?" Up went finger number two. "During which we are free to chill on the decks and use the virtual gaming room and climb the rock wall and, like, go to the spa?" Finger three jumped to attention. "Whenever we want?"

"Almost whenever. There are a few strings."

"What are they?" Jiggy asked, sounding wholeheartedly unconcerned. Clearly my worst-case-scenario mind-set was more pronounced than hers, because I was picturing the so-called STRINGS as shackles.

Dad slid back in his chair and lifted one ankle to rest on top of his other knee. "Well, we'll need to get both of you registered for the college-work shadowing program. Today."

DUHHHH, not only was his statement in no way connected to Jiggy's question, but wasn't he forgetting something HUGE? "Uh, yeah. Sorry to throw a wrench in your grand plan, Dad, but we haven't graduated from high school yet."

"The program's for high school students, Cam. Not to worry. You've already been provisionally accepted."

"Oh." Sorta cool. "But what does that have to do with using the ship's facilities? Get to the strings part."

"Well, obviously you won't be able to use the facilities while you're working, which will be, essentially, four hours a day, five days a week, at your assigned jobs. And you'll need to either write a term paper about the experience or design a creative project by the end of the summer and turn it in to your advisor."

Jiggy and I blinked at each other in confusion. We had to write PAPERS? OVER SUMMER VACATION? What the . . .?

He raised his eyebrows hopefully. "Before you get too disappointed, keep in mind that you'll earn three college credits, which you can transfer to the university you choose after next year. You'll be ahead of the pack on day one of your freshman year."

"Oh!" Jiggy and I said together as our lightbulbs clicked on simultaneously. My bummed-out mood dissipated fully. I dug the idea of being ahead.

"That's awesome!" Jigs added. "It's kind of like getting paid after all."

"Yeah," I said. "I mean, you can't buy Lucky Brand jeans with college credits, but still."

"Totally fair trade-off," Jiggy said.

Dad smiled at Jiggy and visibly relaxed. "I take it you're not too disappointed, then?"

"No way!" Jiggy said, grinning.

Dad raised his eyebrows at me, hopefully.

I laughed, feeling lighter than I had since the day I'd learned of Brett's evilness. "Gee, Dad. Put yourselves in our position and you figure it out. We get to go on a cruise vacation for three months. HELLO! I feared we'd be cleaning staterooms fifteen hours a day."

He lowered his chin and leveled me with the obligatory parental nag stare. "Vacation or not, let's not forget your SAT studying, Camille. I'll expect you to put in two hours a day on top of your job. No fooling around. I'll be checking in with you—and so will Maurice—to make sure you're keeping up."

Studying. I hated Brett anew, but I hiked my chin with

defiance. "I haven't forgotten, Dad. Give me a little credit. I'm not going to screw up the test again, believe me."

He held up both hands, as if in surrender.

Appeased, I asked, "Can I study in a deck chair?"

Dad shrugged, then nodded. "A couple other things. While you're working, I expect you to represent the ship in a manner that will make the captain proud. You won't be uniformed as crew members, but that's irrelevant. Understood?"

We nodded obediently.

He waved a hand in front of his face. "This is me switching from captain mode to dad mode."

"Whoo-boy," I said, on an exhale. "Let me guess: This is part of the bad news, too?"

Dad just chuckled. "When you're not working, I expect you to represent yourselves in a manner that will make your parents, Jiggy, and Camille, your mom and me proud. I guess I don't have to tell you that I don't want you drinking or sneaking into the casino or bringing people . . . well, boys . . . back to your stateroom."

"No problem," Jiggy said, with this totally serious expression on her face. "Just grown men, then? Like, over age thirty, or what?"

"You." Dad play-smacked her in the head, and she giggled.

I ignored the drinking and sneaking provisions (yeah, yeah, yeah—same parental nags, different locale), fixating fully on the GUYS part. "Guys in our room—young or old—isn't something you have to stress about on my account, Dad," I said, with a giant scoff and a humongous eye-roll. "In case you've completely forgotten, I'm OUT of that game."

"I haven't forgotten, honey." Dad reached across the table to tug on my earlobe. "But I don't want you to let one bad experience ruin this summer for you."

"Duh! What no one seems to grasp is that staying away from guys will *make* my summer, not ruin it."

He looked skeptical. "A cruise is an escape. Take advantage of it and forget Brett, if that's what you need to do. You'll meet a lot of nice kids every week on the cruises, and we have some fine young crew members, too."

I set my jaw stubbornly. "So? This isn't 1950. Nice or not, their mere presence in my airspace doesn't mean I am required to date them."

Dad angled his chin down in agreement. "No, it doesn't. But you can have fun. Make friends. Even with boys."

"Blech."

He sighed. "Look. I know how teenage boys think. You girls have my sympathy in that respect. But not all of them are bad eggs."

I remained stonily silent.

"Just try, Cammie," Dad said softly. "I hate to see you embittered at seventeen."

Greaaaaaat. That sounded like the title to a bad after-school special: "Embittered at Seventeen," starring Camille Tafoya. How perfectly horrid. "Can we just stop talking about my personal life now, please, before I vomit mango smoothie all over your pristine white captain shoes?"

"As long as you promise me you'll try," Dad said, choosing to ignore my grossness.

"She will," Jiggy assured him.

I burned her a major stink eye. "Fine. I'll try," I said, in a totally "screw that" tone of voice. The truth is, I wouldn't, but I was sick of defending my position. No one got it. How could I ever trust a guy again? But it wasn't even that—not completely, at least. The bigger question was, how could I trust *myself*? My own instincts? I'd disgraced myself with the whole Brett thing, and I needed to prove, mostly to myself, that I had better judgment than that. I might play like the queen of cool sarcasm, but my self-esteem was at an all-time, bottom-feeder, mud-sucking low. And, my GOD, I had to spend another whole year with all the kids at school who thought I'd eagerly bumped uglies with Brett Mason . . . a guy way out of my league who hadn't even LIKED me.

I was *embarrassed*, okay? Putting myself in the position of trusting again, risking again, being thrown under the bus again just made me feel panicky, not to mention about as desirable as a monster forehead zit on senior picture day. It wasn't just that I wanted to avoid guys this summer—I NEEDED to. I needed to feel empowered and in control. Also, confident—in my abilities to rock the SAT, my skill for reading guys correctly—all of it. I needed the old Camille back, better and stronger and tougher then KEVLAR. But I didn't bother trying to explain any of that to my dad or Jiggy.

Apparently satisfied with my lame promise, Dad

slapped both palms down on his knees. "Okay, then. I'm so glad we were able to work this out, girls. I'm looking forward to having you around this summer."

"Thank you for saving us from Tanzania and Argentina," Jiggy said.

Dad grinned. "*De nada*, although I'm sure you two would have enjoyed those experiences too."

SNORT! Not.

"If you two don't have any other immediate questions," he said in this weird hinting way that made my brain go HUH?!, "I need to get back to work."

"We're cool," I said, not sure what he was getting at, which was nothing new.

"O-o-okay, then." Dad stood. "Maurice will show you to your stateroom and help you get settled in."

"I like Maurice. He's funny," Jiggy said, and I nodded my agreement.

Maurice has this perfect, British demeanor, but beneath it lurks a hilarious snarkiness I am totally down with. He's always making bitchy little comments out of the side of his mouth that no one would ever expect from him. It rules.

Dad smiled. "He's a good man, and he'll be available to you whenever you need something and can't get to me."

"So, can we, like, explore the ship now?" Jiggy asked.

"Sure. I can have Maurice give you a tour, if you'd like."

"That's okay," I told him quickly. "We'd rather explore on our own."

"That's fine. There won't be any passengers until tomorrow, so you two just enjoy yourselves, but try to stay out of the crew members' way while they set up. I'll make sure you're introduced to your job mentors after we set sail."

"What's a job mentor?" Jiggy asked.

He opened his mouth, then closed it again. "I'll keep it simple. They're your supervisors. They'll show you the ropes of your assigned jobs, take you under their wings."

I suddenly realized what piece of this giant puzzle was missing. I reached out and touched Jiggy's arm while looking at my dad. "Wait one freakin' minute. We forgot to ask the most important question. Where exactly will we be working?" *Please let it not be on the housekeeping staff!*

A slow, mischievous grin transformed my dad's face. He blew out a breath and did this geeky, fake wiping-sweat-from-his-brow gesture. "Well, it's about time. I thought you'd never ask."

"You weren't going to tell us until we asked?" I said, my voice squeaky with disbelief.

"Hey, dads want to have a little fun too. Let's call this part of the good news." He smoothed his palms together. "Miss Jiggy will be working in Vibe, our Internet café, in the computer section, of course."

Jiggy's eyes bugged like only a true computer geek's can, and I say that with love. "Seriously? Sweet! Ohmigod. Thank you SO much!"

He reached across and tugged my earlobe again. He'd always done that, since I was a toddler. "And you, my little spider girl, will work on the fitness deck. How does working as a belay monkey on the rock-climbing wall sound?"

"WHAT?" I shot straight out of my chair and threaded the fingers of both hands into my hair. I loved—and I mean LOVED—rock-wall climbing. I'd gotten hooked on it in Boulder and continued it regularly at the indoor rock gym in Madison.

Dad smiled. "I told you we didn't intend to ruin your vacation, girls. Ye of little faith. We want you to have jobs you'd enjoy. So. Think you can have a fun summer now, even though you're stuck with boring old me?" His eyes gleamed as if he totally knew the answer to *that* question.

We both flung ourselves into my dad's arms for a giant bear hug, the exact kind Jiggy never shared with her own father. I felt a pang of sympathy for her, while at the same time silently retracted all the uncharitable thoughts I'd ever had about my own dad. Or at least the ones from today. He had completely hooked us UP. Working at the rock wall for four hours a day wouldn't even feel like work!

A few minutes later, as I followed Jiggy, who followed Maurice down the skinny little companionway toward our ninth-deck stateroom, I squeezed my eyes shut and thanked the universe for this complete luck turnaround. Our lives may not be perfect, but the prospects for summer fun were definitely looking up. The end of the school year had sucked the big wazoo, no doubt about it. But, we'd survived. I'd even escaped Madison without running into Brett again. Now it was OUR turn to have good karma on our side. We *deserved* it.

I sincerely hoped all the bad karma had stuck around

in Madison, waiting to bite ol' Brett and his cronies on their nasty, lying asses, which is exactly what *they* deserved. If there was any justice in the world, Jiggy and I would have the best summer ever while the gaggle of virgin baggers suffered three months of pure misery, complete with poison ivy, body lice, acne, mono, heat stroke, B.O., jock itch, speeding tickets, hemorrhoids, and every other unpleasant thing the universe could possibly dream up to throw their way.

Yeah, I know. Evil wishes like that weren't exactly good for my own karmic upkeep. Try as I might, though, I couldn't make myself take them back.

chapter five

As promised, our stateroom ruled.

It had two skinny little twin beds, an itty-bitty bathroom (with a toilet that vacuum-flushed so freakin' hard, it could suck the contacts right off your eyeballs if you weren't careful, but that's a whole 'nuther topic), and our own private balcony, which was the best part. We had a good five-minute wig session over that. We never even DREAMED our home-away-from-home would rock so fully.

But, cool as it was, we didn't want to spend all our time stuck in the room. Especially now that we knew the whole ship was ours for the taking. We unpacked quickly, changed into our cutest not-trying-too-hard-to-look-cute outfits, carefully fixed our hair and makeup to look like we hadn't bothered because we were so naturally perfect that we didn't need to, then set off to explore.

Everywhere we went, crew members bustled around readying the ship for tomorrow's onslaught of passengers. No one even really noticed us as far as I could tell. Everyone seemed to be working really hard, but there was a lot of joking around and laughter too. Totally fun atmosphere. Much to my surprise, none of them appeared too bummed out that they had to work like a prison chain gang for the next however many months. I guess that's a prime example of location, location, location making all the difference in the world. Being shackled to your job for the majority of your waking hours was, apparently, A-OKAY as long you did it on the open seas. Who knew?

The ship was like a floating city, with shops, restaurants—everything you could possibly need. Jigs and I traipsed through the bowling alley, then checked out the skating rink and a couple of dance clubs—closed, of course. We made a long, slow circle through the shopping pavilion, peeked into the off-limits casino and several bars and restaurants. We squealed over every deck and pool we came to, and then we headed toward Vibe, the Jigster's soon-to-be work domain. Maurice had given us a little map and circled where it was. After Vibe, we planned to check out the climbing wall, and I could hardly wait!

Vibe turned out to be easy to find but totally hard to wrap our brains around. We both stopped dead in the doorway, all slackjawed; this place was way wicked cooler than any coffee shop I'd ever seen. I mean, KILLER. It had a bright, funky retro feel, with a full-service barista station and smoothie bar, low, groovy-shaped seating pits, and beyond all that, row after row of shiny computers for passengers (and us!) to use at will.

When I recovered from my own awe, I smacked my best friend in the stomach with the back of my hand, hoping she would remember to breathe. "Dude," I said reverently.

Jiggy released a long sigh and clasped her hands in front of her chest, as if in prayer. "Oh, my God, this is so awesome, I feel like I'm going to faint," she said, on a gushy exhale.

"Don't do that," I teased. "They'll think you can't handle it and put you on housekeeping duty. You'll have to scrub those freaky brain-sucker toilets all day long."

"Very funny. Don't distract me." She flicked me away as if I were an annoying buzzy insect and moved into the place a few steps. "I'm worshipping at the temple of technology." She crossed over to one of the computers, ran her fingers reverently along the pristine keyboard, and then brightened and turned back toward me. "Hey! If our work schedules don't coincide, maybe you can do some of your studying in here during my hours!"

I shrugged. "Sure." But I secretly hoped our schedules *did* mesh. I'm not a wallflower or anything, but I didn't exactly dig the idea of bumming around the ship by myself. "Maurice said there's an awesome library on the top deck, too, with 360-degree views of the ocean."

"Man. Don't you wish we had that at school?"

School. I made a face. "Ugh, must you remind me of that hellmouth?" Immediately I thought of—well, you know.

"I'm sorry, Cam. I didn't mean to . . ." She jammed her arms crossed and scowled.

I blinked at her, kind of surprised. "Are you mad?"

"Yes." She paused. "But not at you. At Brett."

I held up a hand. "Ix-nay on the ett-Bray talk before I arf-bay, thank you very uch-may."

"I know. And I won't keep talking about the whole situation—or him—I promise. But I just have to vent for a sec, okay? Please?"

"Fine. Ignore my trauma. Vent away," I said, with a sigh, knowing the sooner she talked about him, the sooner she'd stop talking about him, hence, the sooner I'd stop wanting to hurl.

She paced back and forth. "I mean, it's just unfair."

"Duh."

"Be quiet. Let me finish."

"Fine." I rolled my hand.

"Here we are in hottie central for the next three solid, sun-drenched months, and you've sworn off guys."

"So?"

She gaped. "What do you mean, 'so'? If he hadn't pulled his crap, we could launch a world-class, no-holds-barred flirt fest this summer."

"In actuality, if he hadn't" —I made air quotes with my fingers—"pulled his crap, I probably would've studied, most likely would've scored well on the SAT, and we wouldn't be here at all."

"Well . . . yeah, if you want to get technical about it. But, still." She waved away the TRUTH (HELLO?!?) with her hand, then spun toward me with her arms spread wide. "The point remains: this is a once-in-a-lifetime, target-rich environment, Cam, and it just blows that we can't take advantage of it."

"*You* can."

She rolled her eyes. "Boy-hunting's not half as much fun alone, and you know it."

I didn't argue her point, but I wasn't willing to cave, either. I slipped one foot out of my new beaded flip-flops—which were doing that new-shoe-pain thing between my toes—and rested one bare foot on top of the other while waiting for her to get it all out of her system.

She blew out an angry breath that lifted the wisps of hair off her forehead. "I just feel . . . I don't know. Like Brett got away with everything."

I sort of laughed, but not because anything was remotely funny. "Uh, yeah. That's because he did."

"That's what I'm saying. He didn't even learn his lesson."

"Well . . . there's nothing I can do about it."

"That's so wrong. There has to be something—"

"There isn't, so we might as well just forget it."

She pondered this, finally blowing out a breath. "And, to top it off, he jacked up your whole shipboard romance mojo."

Now, there was a laugh riot. "News flash, Jigs: I've never had romance mojo in my life, shipboard or otherwise."

She ignored me. "For all we know, the jerk is out there right this minute deflowering another unsuspecting virgin—"

"Jiggy!" I rasped, and then glanced around before lunging toward her. I clutched her wrist and lowered my voice. "For God's sake, watch what you're saying! I may have a few petals missing, but I am not deflowered!"

"You know what I'm saying, Cam. It's just so . . . unfair."

"Well, nobody ever said life would be fair," I snapped, frustrated and sounding creepily parental, even to myself.

She ignored that truth as well, deep into her indignation, by this point. "I mean, did you get a load of all those hot, hot, HOT crew guys?"

Not this again. My chin jutted out. "Uh, look, Jiggy. I'm sorry you're bummed—truly. And I agree that Brett deserves worse than he got. But I wasn't checking out the hot crew guys, and I have no interest in doing so at all this summer."

Okay, it was a partial lie.

I *wasn't* interested in hooking up with any of them. That part was true. But it's hard not to notice sun-bronzed and built hotties speaking French and Italian and Spanish, etc., to each other, muscles flexing as they set up deck chairs and tables and stuff. I mean, I have hormones just like every other unfortunate girl. In truth, the whole meandering-through-the-hotties sitch had been rather torturous. But after the first few alarming minutes, I'd worked out a plan in my head: Every time a given crew god made my tummy flutter, I forced myself to superimpose Brett's face over his, and the flutters stopped quicker than a butterfly slamming into the windshield of a semi. Flutter-BYE, know what I mean?

"The whole summer," Jiggy said, with a tone of disbelief.

"Yes." I crisscrossed my hands in front of me. "Bottom line, there is no way in hell I'm setting myself up for another fall. Not looking, not noticing, not interested."

Jiggy pinned me with a droll stare. "Come on. Remember who you're talking to, here. I know you."

"Meaning what?"

"Meaning, because you're allegedly not interested, you're suddenly blind? You can honestly stand there and tell me you didn't even *see* any of them?" she asked, using the old answering-a-question-with-a-sarcastic-question-of-your-own tactic.

I pushed out a harassed and growly sigh. Dude. This whole conversation was a total buzzkill, and just when we were starting to have some fun on the ship. "Look," I said, feeling the heat rising inside me the more pissed off I became. "No, I'm not blind, okay? But you have no idea how much I wish I were. I don't care how hot these crew guys are, and YES, I've noticed that they are—"

"Ha! I knew—"

"BUT—" I cut her off, jamming my point-making finger straight up in the air between us, "at the risk of repeating myself *ad nauseam*, none of this matters in the long run, because GUYS SUCK. All of them. Even the hot ones. Maybe especially the hot ones! They suck harder than the stupid toilet in our freakin' stateroom, okay. Now, can we please drop it and go see the rest of the ship before I have to throw myself overboard to end this tedious conversation?"

Without waiting for her answer, I spun around and slammed face-first into the chest of one of the aforementioned crew gods.

"Hey-yo. You okay?" He grabbed my arms to steady me.

I blinked up at him, totally dazed. My whole face hurt from the blow my nose took against his toned pecs, and I could feel my eyes start to water profusely. I reached up to un-deviate my septum, praying I wouldn't start gushing blood. He must've walked in behind me while I was ranting, which sucked. Crap, how much had he overheard?

"Are you hurt? Aw, don't cry." He touched my arm gently, the warmth of his hand sending zingers through me.

I eased my arm away from him with as much dignity as I could muster, then averted my gaze. "I'm not crying," I said, with a tinge of annoyance in my tone. "My eyes are watering. That happens when you break your nose."

His expression morphed into what looked like genuine shock and concern. "Holy—your nose is broken?"

My skin suddenly blazed with heat. "Uh, well . . . no. I'm okay. I was being sarcastic. It's a personality flaw. Sorry," I muttered, wiping at my eyes with the back of my hand.

He visibly relaxed, then laid one palm on his chest. His muscular, sexy chest, I'm loath to add, which was attached to wide shoulders and ripped, tanned arms. SHUT UP, CAMILLE! God, I was more pathetic then I even realized.

"I should've watched where I was going. My bad." He sort of tilted his chin down, cupped my elbows—which jerked my gaze up to his face—then studied me through his long, black lashes. "Sure you're all right?"

Whoa-Nelly. His eyes were this sort of deep amber color, and he had a dimple in the left side of his cheek. His perfectly tousled black hair looked like he styled it simply by surfing every morning. He epitomized a bona fide island boy, with a sun-bronzed face so open and friendly, I had a hard time superimposing Brett's vile visage over it. It seemed so wrong. Instead, I stepped back, feeling off-kilter and pissed at myself for feeling off-kilter, especially on the heels of my quite impressive anti-guy speech. Totally destroyed the impact of my righteous indignation when I got all girly-stupid over the first guy I ran into—literally. Let's face it: A guy like this wouldn't even be speaking to me if I hadn't crashed into him. A wave of self-consciousness broke over me, leaving me sputtering and uncertain in its wake. I could hardly lift my eyes. "I-it's okay. Really. It was my fault, anyway. Let's . . . uh . . . go, Jiggy."

I started toward the door, but stopped when I heard *cabaña* boy let out a surprised laugh. I looked back just as he grinned at my best friend.

"Your name's Jiggy? For real?"

Jiggy nodded and smiled.

"That's a great name."

"Thanks. It's really just a nickname. My real name is too embarrassing for words. Well, the story behind it, at least, if not the actual . . . never mind."

Jiggy rambles when she's nervous. It's actually quite endearing. But at that moment, I wished she'd get a handle on her nerves so we could get the hell out of there.

I took one more step toward the door, and then—

"Embarrassing, huh? I'll tell you mine if you tell me yours," he said to Jiggy, all flirty like, obliterating my hopes that this hellish encounter would end anytime soon.

I could hardly hold back the eye-roll, but to spite me, my stomach got all soury feeling. It felt like jealousy, but HELLO! Why would I be jealous? Point A: Jiggy and I were never jealous of each other; and point B: I wanted nothing to do with this guy. I didn't even KNOW him. Not to mention the fact that he wouldn't want anything to do with me, either. And why wouldn't island boy flirt with Jiggy? Clearly she didn't exude virgin-in-need-of-a-pity-lay vibes like Yours Truly. I hugged my arms around my middle, wishing I could just disappear. Oblivious to my inner torment, their conversation rolled on.

"No chance." But Jiggy held out her hand to him. "I am, and will always be, simply Jiggy. Yearling. Jiggy Yearling, that is. Nice to meet you . . . ?"

"Makaio," he said, pronouncing it like muh-KY-oh. "Makaio Ulloa." They shook hands, and then he peered over at me. "And the name of your friend who thinks all guys suck?" He chuckled softly. "That toilet comment was pretty funny, yah?"

My face flamed again. He *had* heard me. That blew. But, oh well, at least now that he knew my true feelings, he'd avoid me like an STD, which would save me from having to avoid him. And he hadn't been around to hear the deflowering part, thank God for small favors.

"I'm Camille," I muttered finally, pulling my fingers away from my disjointed nose. I checked for blood before reluctantly shaking his hand. If the fact that I used my nosebleed-stopping hand for the shake grossed him out, too damn bad.

"Don't mind the attitude. Camille's having a bad day. So, you work on the ship, I take it?" Jiggy asked, stepping casually between me and Makaio. "I mean, obviously. Duh," she added, with her back in my face, full-on blowing me off and cutting me out of the convo in one slick move.

I supposed I'd asked for that. I mean, I could reframe it: Jiggy was saving me from having to make stupid small talk with him, since I'd made it more than clear I wanted no guy contact. Whatever. I sidled away, pretending deep interest in a display of Tazo tea bags, but I couldn't refrain from monitoring Jiggy and the bohunk Hawaiian guy with my peripheral vision.

He nodded. "Every summer while I'm in college, hopefully. This is my second year." He aimed his thumb toward a computer. "I was just gonna check my e-mail really quick. I'm on a break."

"Oh, sure." Jiggy stepped aside so he could head toward the computers. "So, where do you work?"

"I'm an instructor on the fitness deck." He sat on a computer stool and clicked open his mail program, typing with all ten fingers, which I knew would earn him points in Jiggy's book. While his e-mail list loaded, he sat back. "What about you two? I don't remember you from last summer."

Back the hell up!

DID HE SAY HE WORKED ON THE FITNESS DECK?

My stomach lurched violently, and against my volition, I spun toward them, no doubt with a open-mouthed, horrified expression on my face.

THE FREAKIN' FITNESS DECK?

THE HOTTIE WHO OVERHEARD ME COMPARING GUYS TO TOILETS WORKED ON THE FITNESS DECK?! How damn MURPHY'S LAW-esque was that? My life plummeted to a new low.

"Hey! Camille will be working on the fitness deck!" Jiggy innocently announced, unaware of or ignoring my shock and horror.

Makaio smiled, then lifted his chin toward me. "Yah?"

I nodded, then managed to snap my jaw closed through sheer force of will.

"*Shaka.* That's cool."

I crossed my arms, using the time to regain my composure—what little of it was left. "Well, we're . . . uh . . . not even really working on the ship."

A line of confusion bisected his forehead. "Say what?"

I shifted impatiently from one foot to the other. "Never mind. It's a long, stupid story. Trust me, you don't want to hear it, so don't let us keep you from your e-mail."

He didn't move, instead raising one eyebrow quizzically.

I pressed my lips together momentarily to keep from yelling out a big, humongous ARGH! "It's just . . . some college thing," I said, impatiently. "Hard to explain . . ." I let my voice trail off and peered over at the door.

"Hold up."

To my surprise, Makaio took a step toward me, his eyes suddenly bright and curious.

"Are you Captain Tafoya's daughter?"

I managed a shocked little squeak, but I couldn't make anything intelligible come out. How could he possibly TELL?

"She is," Jiggy said, all happy about it.

"H-how'd you know that?" I stammered.

Makaio shrugged in this casual way that inadvertently made his shoulder muscles flex. Evil, evil. "Because, as far as I know, there are only two students in the program this summer, and one of them—the captain's daughter—is scheduled to work on the fitness deck." He tapped one finger on his temple, obviously proud of his keen deductive powers.

For some reason, his answer annoyed me. "Geez, what is it? Front-page news?" I forked my fingers through the sides of my hair, exasperated with the whole thing. I'd come on the ship hoping to escape my unwanted and undeserved notoriety, and now it seemed as though people were already talking about me here. It never ended. "I suppose the entire crew knows every little detail about my life," I snapped (sort of unfairly, but remember? LIFE ISN'T FAIR!).

"Nah. Nothing like that. Most people probably don't even know you're here."

"Oh, no?" I said, in a snarky tone.

He shook his head. "Seriously. Not even about the

college program, really. It's new, so it's pretty much on the down low, eh."

I tried to narrow my gaze and look tough, but had to glance away quickly. Dangit. Makaio Ulloa was one of those guys it seemed hard to look at for more than a few seconds at a time without becoming all . . . chickish. YECH. "If it's so on the DL, then how'd you manage to find out?"

"They had to tell me." He paused just long enough to pique my curiosity and make me look back up into his face. When I did, he crossed his arms over his chest and let his mouth spread slowly into a smile.

"Had to? Why?" I blurted.

"Because I'm your job mentor."

My heart spasmed. No freakin' way.

HOT. ISLAND. BOY. WAS. MY. JOB. MENTOR?!

Holy—! Time didn't grind to a stop, like you always read about it books. Oh, no. It crashed to a halt in one ugly instant, like a train hitting the side of a mountain and bursting into flame.

I plunked down on the edge of a nearby sofa, because my legs had gone rubbery, and pondered this new tragic reality. Unless this was just one, long nightmare, it appeared I was stuck on this ship for three months—the same three months during which I'd hoped to hide out, kill off my hormones, and grow a shell hard enough to protect me from the evils of guys, mind you—working alongside Makaio Ulloa, a hormone-tripping, resolve-dissolving guy if there ever was one. A guy who threatened to make all memories of the Brett debacle fade away until I tripped stupidly down the path of self-destruction once again.

GLUG. I was so screwed.

"Oh . . . well . . . huh." I managed to give Makaio a sick smile and realized, suddenly, that I should've been much, MUCH nicer to the karma gods.

www.NobodyGetsJiggy.com

The Goddess, here, coming at you cyber-live from Hawaii. ALOHA!!!!!!!!!! Looks like No Problemo to keep on bloggin' over the summer, since I have the most righteous job EV-ER in the ship's Internet café. Everything here rocks so far—more than either my BF or I expected it to. I'd started to worry that this summer, which was supposed to be the best ever, was actually going to blow because of my BF's boring three-pronged summer plan: studying, celibacy, and self-esteem building. But I think I may have found a secret weapon to use against her (because I just can't let her set herself up for regret like that).

His name is—LIKE I'M GOING TO TELL YOU! You know the blog rules. We'll call him M. The best part is, C can't avoid M, because he's sort of her boss, in a way (long story). And he seems really, really nice—not B-like at all. Plus, trust me, M has caught C's eye, even if she won't admit it. A BF can tell these things. Stay tuned for updates, 'cuz I'm sure there will be lots to tell, trust me on that one.

Gotta fly! Tomorrow is my first workday, and I haven't even met my boss yet.

Smooches, The Goddess of NobodyGetsJiggy.com

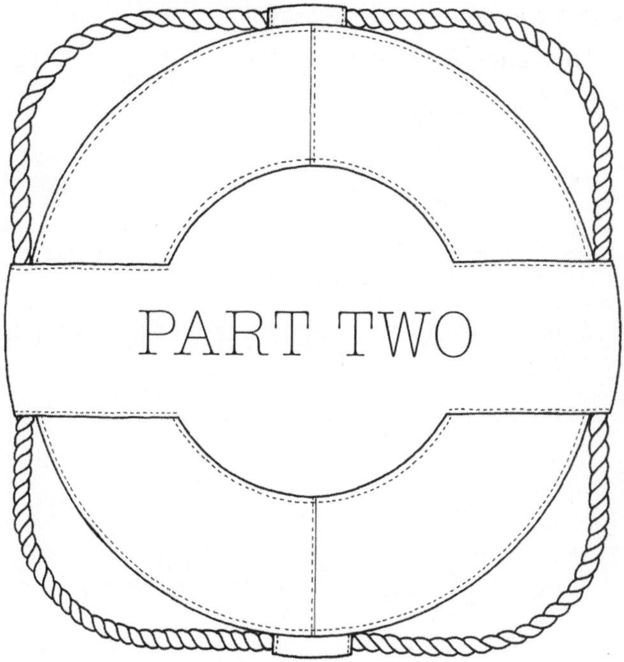

PART TWO

chapter six

"So then he totally ditched her *at* the altar," Jiggy whispered to me from her deck chair, which was squished up next to mine so we could talk without disrupting the Teen Meet & Greet going on around us.

"No. Way. Seriously?"

"Uh-huh." For a sec, we just stared at each other in disbelief across our umbrella drinks—passion fruit piña coladas, virgin, of course. A gentle, early evening breeze swirled Jiggy's hair around her face. One honey strand looped across her chin, but she pushed it away. I swear, Jiggy's gorgeous mane already looked perfectly sun-streaked, the lucky wench, while my brown tangle just looked puffier and even less controllable than usual.

But hair issues SO did not compare to what Jiggy's job mentor, Lani, had gone through. Ditched at the freakin' altar? "That . . . *blows*," I murmured. "I mean, more than blows. It's like . . ." I shook my head. There weren't words, really. Suffice it to say, my Brett wounds, deep as they felt, were mere scrapes compared to Lani's love amputations.

Beyond the decks, the ocean spread out around us like a bed of gilded jade. Everything smelled like sunshine, salt water, and supreme relaxation. Right then, life truly felt hand-dipped in perfection.

Unless you were Lani.

I bit my knuckle, reeling from it all.

"Yeah, so, anyway—"

"Wait," I interrupted. "She's how old again?"

"Twenty-four."

"Crap. Young. She's gone through twenty-four lifetimes' worth of hell already, if you ask me."

Jiggy blew out this unamused bark of a laugh. "Um, yeah. And you don't know the half of it yet, because I'm not even finished."

"There's more? Tell me!"

"I'm trying to." She crossed one leg over the other and bounced her foot—bare except for about six silver-and-bead anklets twinkling on her right ankle. "Dude, not only did he chuck her under the bus on her own wedding day, but the only explanation was a message on her cell phone saying he loved someone else. And not even, 'I'm so sorry, I love someone else.' Just, flat out, 'I love someone else.'"

"Asshole! That's so typical." Like I knew. Snort.

She bugged her eyes. "God, I *hope* that's not typical. I can't even imagine the embarrassment of standing there, a hundred-some-odd guests staring at you with pity while you check your voice mail. Can you?" She shuddered, then rubbed her upper arms as if chilled.

Thing was, I sort of *could* imagine it. The TRAUMA of it, at least. Pity, scorn, dislike, shame, gossip. So totally. I sipped my colada, glancing toward the front of the lounge to make sure our whispering wasn't annoying the cruise directors. I didn't want to piss off any of the crew and send someone running to my dad. Luckily, no one seemed to have noticed. I felt a small pang of guilt for full-on blowing this shindig off, but catching up with Jiggy was much more important. We'd survived our first shifts at "work," and hadn't had a single moment to fill each other in on the details. Until now.

"So, when did this wedding happen? Or not happen?"

She lowered her chin, leveling me with a stare. "Ready?"

I cringed. "I'm not sure."

"Valentine's Day."

"Dude!"

"I know!"

"Now he's destroyed her Valentine's Day basically forever." I clonked my drink down on the table next to me. "Why do people have to DO that kind of stuff on a major holiday?"

"Who knows?" She shrugged. "I vote for, he's a complete jerk who deserves to be shark bait?"

"Indeed."

"But, wait! There's more," she said in an informercial voice, jabbing one finger in the air.

"You have GOT to be making this up."

"Not. Shark bait actually married the other woman in March, and . . . brace yourself."

I gripped the armrests of my chair.

"She had their baby this month."

"No!"

"Cross my heart, hope to die." She made needle-jabbing motions toward her eye.

It was all so shocking, I felt I needed to confirm what I *thought* I'd heard. I leaned forward and laid my hand on her leg. "You're telling me this other chick was actually PREGNANT while the idiot planned a wedding with Lani?"

"Fully. But it gets worse." She waited while I flopped back in my chair. "Three weeks after that, Lani got laid off and had to sell the condo they were *supposed* to have lived in together. At a loss."

I stared at her, stunned. It really was too much. "Jigs, that's like awful overkill. Awful to the tenth power. Awful-gone-haywire."

Jiggy ran one hand through the top of her hair. "Yeah. Her first computer programming job out of college, too, and the hiring process was unbelievably competitive, I guess. She was crushed." She flipped one hand over. "So, anyway, long story long, that's why she's here. To get away from all that. She said she didn't mind having to sell their place, because it reminded her of Steve. But, the rest of it . . ."

"Man, another evil guy ruining another trusting girl's

life. Same story, different cast." My stomach swirled, and NATURALLY, I thought of Brett. Tension consumed me. I tried to relax and soak in the last rays of golden sun, but Lani's tale of woe had me freaked. We'd set sail the night before, and we'd been at sea all day. I could completely understand Lani choosing to escape her reality by working on the ship, now that we'd gotten a taste of the strange but really cool lifestyle. It felt like a whole different universe out here, removed from the regular hectic pace of life on land. I could hardly remember what Madison even felt or looked like.

"How's she handling it all? Is she, like, suicidal?" I bit my bottom lip.

"Nope. Hardly." Jigs pulled her knees up to her chest and wrapped her arms around them. She wore a long-sleeved, coral cover-up with crocheted cuffs that almost covered her hands. "I mean, she's bitter. Duh. But she seems so strong. She deals much better than I think I would."

I thought about how my own bitterness seemed to eat at me like acid, and felt a little ashamed. What made Lani so much stronger?

A small smile teased at the corners of Jiggy's lips. "She's hilarious, though. She comes up with all these awesome revenge plans while we're working. Like, whacked out, unbelievable stuff."

"How cool!"

Jiggy reached for her drink, stirred it with the tiny little umbrella handle, then sipped. "Yeah. Every so often she'll look over and say, 'Hey, Jiggy. What do you think of this idea?'"

"Wow." My eyes widened with respect. "Do you think she'll carry through with any of them?"

"Nah, but I told her she should write a screenplay. She'd be a bazillionaire." She chuckled, shaking her head. "I think it just makes her feel better to imagine all this horrible karmic retribution for the idiot."

"I'm totally feeling her on the revenge and karmic retribution concepts," I said, with a sigh. If life were fair (and, of course, we've already established that it is NOT), I would've been assigned to work with Lani instead of her being partnered with Jiggy. Dude, I SO could've used a dose of her snarky medicine.

But, no—my own workday flashed through my brain.

Instead, I got stuck with the most sought-after crew guy on the ship, apparently, and being around him just made me doubt myself and my judgment even more. DAY ONE, and already my success hopes were dwindling, bitterness was turning me into an evil shrew, and I wasn't even confident enough to plot a screenplay-worthy death for Brett.

I sucked.

Jigs drained her drink with a quick, loud slurp, licked off the umbrella handle, then set everything aside. "So. I told you everything I know so far. Your turn. How was your first day at the rock wall?"

Bleh. THAT. And Makaio. I knew I wouldn't be able to avoid this conversation forever. You know, it would've been so much easier to hate the guy if he'd been overtly cocky or flirtatious or Brettesque . . . something. But he hadn't been. He was just regular old nice, all laid back and mellow. Not that I trusted the NICE thing anymore. Still. I reached up and scratched my cheek. "Okay, I guess."

Jiggy blinked at me a couple times, as if waiting for me to expound on the topic. When I didn't oblige, she added, "Um . . . okay. Did you climb?"

"Nah."

She cocked her head and frowned. "Why not? I thought you were dying to climb. The wall is awesome."

Um, because that would've put me in direct contact with Makaio? I shrugged. "Busy?"

"Oh. Well, are you going to like the job, or what?"

I shrugged again. "I guess."

Jigs placed the palm of one hand onto the tips of the other fingers, forming a T. "Time out. I told you Lani's life story, practically, and you've given me SEVEN whole words. Only three if I don't count the 'I guess'es, and I would've gotten NONE if I hadn't badgered you."

"Well, news flash: My job mentor is MALE. I don't know Makaio's life story," I pointed out, "nor do I want to."

"I know *that*, Cam." She rolled her hand. "But what did you do all day? What was he like to work with? Is he nice? Did he say anything?"

"About what?"

"ANYTHING." She made strangling motions in my general direction.

I sniffed and studied my short, bare nails. I needed a manicure. And a pedicure; I peered down at my equally dull toes, wiggling them a bit. "Well, he didn't bring up our auspicious first meeting, if that's what you're asking. Although . . . he did ask how my nose was feeling."

"How sweet!" She bounced into a comfy girl-talk position. "So, what's he like?"

"You met him."

"Yeah, for like two seconds. I want to know what *you* think he's like."

Boy, that was a tough one. I blew out a sigh that weighed about a thousand tons. "Well . . . everybody seems to like him." Understatement of the century.

What I didn't add was that Makaio Ulloa could be the death of my Summer Self-Improvement Plan if I let down my guard for even ONE second. If ever a guy existed who could be deemed The Total Package, Makaio was that guy. Or SEEMED like that guy.

I mean, I cannot even properly convey how absurdly popular he was with cruisers of the female persuasion, and I'm talking ALL ages. Seriously, ONE DAY into the cruise, and his "status" was abundantly clear. He'd drawn eyelash-batting fans from the newlyweds to the nearly deads, and every age below and in between. Freakin' TODDLERS loved the guy. And I've never seen so many grandma-types who suddenly "had always wanted to try rock climbing," hip fractures be damned. It seemed a little creepy, but whatever. If they couldn't fantasize while on a cruise, when COULD they fantasize?

Besides, the grandmas were one thing, but it was the teenage fans who icked me out the most. Watching them was like staring into a mirror, and the reflection was NOT pretty, let me tell you. If I needed the perfect reminder of how easy it was to be snowed into stupidity by a hot guy (and, let's face it, I did), the constant grating sound of their flirtatious TITTERS worked like a charm. Every nauseating TEE-HEE was like a mega-booster-shot of Brett shame. They didn't even give a rat's ass about climbing—I can guarantee you that. They just wanted the instructor. Blech. It's not that I begrudged the guy his HAREM or anything, since he wasn't taking advantage of the situation in any way I could see, but puh-LEASE.

"How about you?" Jiggy pressed. "Do you like him?"

I burnt her a major stink eye.

She growled in frustration. "Not LIKE HIM, like him, for God's sake. I know you're not thinking like that—"

"Finally!" I clasped my hands and shook them toward the heavens.

"I just mean, is it going to be okay working with him? Throw me a bone, here, Camille. Sheesh."

I thought about it, my lips pursed. "Yeah," I said, at last. "It'll work out. He's constantly busy with climbing lessons, so I'm pretty sure I can avoid him."

A big, tense pause ensued.

I eyed Jiggy with my peripheral vision and caught her staring at me. "What?"

"Well . . . ," Jiggy started, cautiously, "maybe you shouldn't."

"Huh?"

"Avoid him, I mean. Maybe a guy like Makaio is just

what you need to prove that not all guys are evil."

And just like that, it felt like someone dumped a big ol' bucket of *pissed-off* over my head, leaving me drenched and sputtering in it. I spread my arms wide. "You can actually *say* that after all you just told me about Lani? How could you possibly know Makaio's not evil?"

She tilted her head to the side. "Come on."

"No." I swung my legs around and sat on the very edge of my chaise, facing Jiggy, then tugged on the hem of my denim mini with righteous indignation. "That's what I don't get. You, all these girls on the ship"—I flipped my hand out toward no one in particular—"even me, with Brett at least. We take one look at a hot guy and cut him all the slack in the world, regardless of what kind of person he might be on the inside. It's pathetic."

"Yeah, but what are we supposed to do? Distrust first, ask questions later?"

"Maybe so! I bet Lani wishes she would've."

"Oh, stop it, Cam—"

"Stop what?" I jabbed a finger toward her, my eyes narrowed. "I'm the one being smart here. We know absolutely *nothing* about Makaio, Jigs. He could be a freakin' serial killer, for all we know. Ted Bundy was good looking and charming, too."

"Geez, overdramatize much?" She rolled her eyes. "You know that's no way to live."

"Really? Because it seems like the *only* safe way to live."

"Don't you have a gut instinct about people?"

"Sure, but my gut seems to be a pathological liar. Or

dumber than dirt. In any case, give me good, healthy suspicion any day."

Stalemate.

Jiggy sighed, then glanced out over the ocean. I sat back on my chaise and crossed my arms tightly over my middle, feeling unsettled. For a minute, I just listened without really hearing as the teen cruise director told everyone where the teens-only pool was, and ticked off some of the events and excursions kids could participate in without their parents.

After what felt like eons of mutual jaw clenching, Jiggy cleared her throat. "So, anyway . . . Lani has the evening off," she said, in a soft voice. Her truce tone. She glanced over at me and tucked her hair behind her ears. "She invited us to come down to her room for a party. Want to go? She's dying to meet you."

My gaze drifted toward the polished wooden deck, and I bit my lip for a sec. I so wanted to accept Jiggy's olive branch; I hated it when we disagreed. But this . . . "I totally want to meet her too. But not tonight, Jigs."

"Why not?"

"I . . . um . . . haven't gotten much studying done yet." I paused. She wasn't buying it. "And you know what my dad said. Two hours a day."

Her hopeful expression dropped. I mean, this was my best friend. She knew classic Camille bull when she heard it. No way I'd study for the two full hours EVERY day.

I inhaled, then blew it out in a long exhale. "Okay, so that's not really it."

"You don't say," she said, sounding like the newly elected Mayor of Sarcasmaville.

I quirked my mouth to the side. "I can't face it yet . . . the whole mingling thing. I know Lani's doing great with her stuff, but I'm still adjusting. I guess I'm not as resilient as she is. Please try and understand."

"I do. It just . . . upsets me."

"You go," I said, even trying to imbue my tone with some real enthusiasm. "I'll join you next time. Maybe. Just . . . give me some time, okay? I'm seriously not trying to be a jerk."

"Okay." She smiled, a little sadly. "And, anyway, you're not a jerk. You just play one on TV."

"Ha-ha. I'm glad you don't think so."

"You really don't mind if I go, though?" She crinkled her nose. "I mean, I think Lani could really be a good friend to both of us this summer. But I'll stay in the room while you study, if you want. You're my first priority."

"You're mine, too, and that's why I don't want to ruin your summer any more than I already have." I made a face, then managed a smile. "Go. Have fun. Be wild. Horrify your parents. No"—I held up a hand—"forget your parents altogether. But make me proud. I plan to live vicariously through you."

"But not forever," she said, reaching over to squeeze my knee as she stood. "Okay?"

I rolled tension from my neck. "No promises."

"You have to try to get past it. I know what happened was so awful—I saw it. But, you're better than that, Cam.

You deserve better than Brett Mason, and you always have. Don't let him take anything else from you."

All of a sudden feeling like I was *thisfreakingclose* to tears. I hiked my chin and swallowed them back. "Yeah, whatever. Just go." Trying to lighten things up, I reached over and smacked her in the leg with the back of my hand. "Hey, if Lani has any good revenge suggestions for me," I joked, "let me know."

She was in the midst of hiking her fake Prada bag onto her shoulder when I said it, and she froze. Her expression totally said LIGHTBULB MOMENT, then she grinned like the Grinch. Uh-oh.

"Now *that* is the best idea I've heard from you in a long time," she said, giving me a thumbs-up as she headed off.

"Dude!" I called after her as she flounced happily toward our stateroom to get ready for her party. "I was only kidding!" She ignored me, like I knew she would.

chapter seven

After Jiggy left, I tried to squeeze in some deck chair studying, but I felt restless and unmoored by myself and couldn't concentrate. All around me, couples snuggled in the rising moonlight, their entwined bodies pressed against the polished teak railings in this most romantic of settings. Laughter rose from groups of sun-bronzed people relaxing around deck tables, enjoying each other's company. A huge sense of loneliness engulfed me, pulling me down, down, down. The sensation was new and unpleasant. I'd never been *needy*, and I didn't want to start now. I *had* to burn off some of this uncharacteristic edginess.

I dumped my books in the stateroom, changed into track shoes, running shorts, and a University of Wisconsin tank top, then headed to the fitness deck to jog around the track. No one else was there. By this time of night, people had long since moved on from fitness to FUN.

I went through SAT vocabulary words in my head as I ran, so I could legitimately count it as study time, but even that didn't Zen me out. After mile three, I gave up and started stretching and cooling down. As I bent over my outstretched leg, I caught a glimpse of my watch. Just a few minutes until the late seating for dinner, which made it the perfect opportunity to bank parental brownie points and go eat dinner with Dad, all of my own volition. And, okay, the truth was, I wanted to be around somebody who knew and loved me. I felt so far removed from everyone and everything familiar, especially with Jiggy out and about.

I showered in record time, then threw on a simple, green, clearance rack sundress that managed to look fancier than it was. Perfect. After twisting my long unruly curls up into a clamp, I slipped into some high-heeled sandals and headed toward dinner. When I entered the main dining room, however, I found another officer occupying my dad's usual spot at the head of the captain's table, with Maurice seated just to his right.

I hesitated on the landing, unsure what to do.

I caught Maurice's eye and made the standard hiked shoulders/bent arms/palms raised WHADDUP? gesture. He lifted his chin toward me, then turned his *GQ* smile on the rest of the table as he spoke. Probably begging off for a moment—duty calls! He could extricate himself from absolutely any situation with panache. It ruled.

In one smooth move, he stood, refolded his napkin, set it next to his plate, and straightened his already perfect jacket. Then he headed my way looking, as always, impeccable in his dress whites.

"Sweetie, you look like a Camillion bucks," he said, by way of a greeting.

"Thanks." I glanced down at my dress, then back up. "I got it on mondo sale. Nineteen bucks."

"Which, of course, you need tell *no one*." One eyebrow arched.

"Oh." I snapped my fingers. "Riiight." We shared a smile. "Um . . . where's Dad? I thought I'd join him for dinner."

"Up on the bridge." He leaned in and lowered his voice. "There's an unexpected patch of weather along our route that he's trying to avoid."

My heart instantly revved and my mouth went dry. "By 'patch of weather,' do you mean, like, a hurricane?"

Maurice's sky blue eyes widened. "Hush your mouth, sister. We don't speak of the H-word on the ship."

I bit my lip to hide a giggle. "Sorry."

"It's just a storm, but, as they say in the south, it's a biggun'. Nastier than a redneck mother-in-law, too."

I grimaced at his description. "But Dad will drive us . . . or whatever . . . around it, right?"

"God, I hope so. Unless we want to see this meal again, if you know what I mean, and all over the ship."

"Ick, Maurice!" I smacked at him, but he dodged the blow, grinning. Then, clearing his throat once, he transformed back into Mr. Decorum before my eyes, slipping his arm into the crook of mine and walking me slowly toward the doors. "Go on up to the bridge." He leaned his head toward mine as he spoke. "I'll let your dad know you're on the way."

"Really? Okay. He won't be too busy?"

Maurice pulled an astonished face. "For his lovely daughter? Don't be crazy."

I knew I was blushing, because my neck felt super hot. Maurice was always a great balm for any girl's ego.

"And where is the perpetually adorable Miss Jiggy this fine evening?"

"Um . . ." Hesitation. I trusted Maurice, but he was the direct line to my dad. I had to remember that. "She's with her job mentor." Hey, it wasn't a lie. "Okay," I said, with perky finality so he wouldn't probe further. "So. I will go up." My stomach growled audibly, and I laid my palm against it. "Oops! Sorry. I just went running."

We stopped just inside the doors to the dining room. "Honey, why didn't you say something? I'll have a meal sent up. What would you like?"

"Hmmm." I tapped my fingers on my chin. Seriously, EVERYTHING was available to eat on a cruise. "Do you think Dad's eaten?"

Maurice pursed his lips in disapproval. My workaholic Dad had a habit of forgetting to eat, and Maurice nagged him almost as much as Mom did. Thank goodness. "Doubtful. I'll send up two meals. With you there, he'll certainly take a bite or two." He extracted a small leather notebook from his pocket and poised an expensive-looking pen over it. "So. What's your pleasure? Filet mignon? Lobster? Ono in crab sauce?"

I crinkled my nose. Ono? Oh, NO. "Um . . . double cheeseburger?"

He rolled his eyes, emitting a dramatic sigh, then stuffed the notebook and pen back into his pocket. "Still growing into your tastebuds, I see."

"I'll have you know the double cheeseburger is an American delicacy."

"Whatever. One double cheese, it is."

"Two. Dad."

"Right. You want fries with that?"

I chuckled. "Wow, so I guess the rumors about you are true?"

His lip twitched slightly. "Which ones?"

"The ones about how you're all that and a bag of fries. *Ronald*," I teased.

"Very funny. And that's Mr. McDonald to you. But, in case you haven't noticed"—he slicked one palm down the opposite sleeve from elbow to wrist, then reversed the motion—"that red-headed bozo has zero fashion taste. Hello, *yellow* jodhpurs? Please. He and I have nothing in common." He pinned me with a fake-hard stare. "So, smartypants, *fries*?"

"Definitely."

He stuck a knuckle in my back and propelled me forward. "Go, go. I'll send up two artery cloggers with all the trimmings. Chocolate shakes, I assume?"

"Not for me." I patted a hand on my tummy. "Diet Pepsi. Have to watch the bikini figure."

"Oh, *of course*. I should've known." Maurice flicked his hand. "Now, get!"

"Don't forget dessert!"

He sucked in the side of his cheek. "Something low-brow, I assume?"

"Yep. Nothing but the worst for me and my pops. Cellophane wrapped, if at all possible."

"Kids," he muttered, as he turned and glided toward the kitchen.

Joking around with Maurice had eased my weird loneliness a bit, but I was still anxious to see my dad. And I couldn't wait to get a glimpse of the storm up ahead—if you could see it, that is. I made my way up to the bridge and knocked on the security door. Locks turned behind the heavy steel, and then my dad peered out and smiled.

"Cammie. Maurice just called and said you were on your way. This is a nice surprise." He stepped aside. "Come on in. To what do I owe this honor?"

"Thanks. I just felt like it."

He kissed the top of my head as I stepped over the threshold and glanced around.

Definitely, this part of the ship was all business, with the big ol' wheel (really! It's there), instrument panels, and navigation stuff, but it was also decorated nicely. My dad performed a lot of marriages up here, on a deck off to one side, so it had to feel posh and inviting. He got a kick out of the fact that every couple married on his bridge went home with a photograph of them smiling up into each other's eyes, the words EMERGENCY BATTERY ROOM printed in red letters on a door behind them.

And, okay, that was kind of amusing.

"Where's your cohort in crime?"

"With Lani. Um, training."

"Training, huh? And here I thought Jiggy knew more than Bill Gates about computers," he joked.

"She does, but . . ." I shrugged. "New job and all. And Lani has a degree in . . . something computery." With the "unexpected patch of weather" looming, I expected Dad to be stressed out, but he appeared calm as ever. I gazed, with a mixture of disappointment and relief, out the huge panoramic windows at the black, black sky melting into the black, black sea. So much for storm chasing, but at least we weren't going to die. "So, what's up?"

"Not much." He smiled, perching on the stool behind the shiny brass and wooden wheel.

I kicked off my sandals and jumped up to sit on a counter nearby. "You don't have to spare me, Dad. I already got the skinny from Maurice."

He looked confused. "What are you talking about?"

"Hello! Aren't we headed straight for Seasickness Cove?" I dangled my feet, making rhythmic bonkbonk . . . bonkbonk sounds with my heels on the lower cupboard.

"Oh, that. Well, I hope we'll miss it." Dad went back to his instrument panel and did some stuff, then winked over at me. "How was your first workday, *M'ija*?"

"Fine," I said in a distracted voice. I SO did not come

here to talk about work, and besides, BIG FREAKIN' STORM!! This didn't feel at all like some of the giant man versus nature movies I'd seen, where everyone ran around all urgent and sweating, yelling at each other. "But, back up. What do you mean, you *hope* we'll miss it? Aren't you the one in charge of steering this tub?"

"Yes and no."

"Meaning?" I pressed, in my borderline annoyed voice, even though I didn't feel annoyed. It was just our pattern. Strangely enough, my dad's usually infuriating communication style actually comforted me right then. I guess I'd needed a dose of the familiarity. Who'da thunk it?

He stared ahead into the darkness beyond the windows, and I arched up trying to see what he saw. The ship's lights reflected off the white foam that cranked up and outward as we cut a path through the water, but that was it. He flicked a glance at me. "Well, how to explain . . . ? You do know that the ship's basically off-course the majority of the time, right?"

I hadn't known. "Really? What's wrong with it?"

He laughed. "Nothing. All ships are the same."

"That's nuts."

"Nah. It's my job to make small corrections over and over until we arrive at our destination, just like we'd planned." He pumped a fist. "You know . . . have faith. Stay the course, and all that."

"Wow, that kind of sucks."

"Interesting that you think so. Why?"

I reached up and pulled the too-tight clamp out of my

hair, letting the curls drift around my shoulders, then scratched the back of my head vigorously. "I don't know. It would be depressing to know you're going the wrong way constantly, and there's nothing you can do about it."

He leaned his head to the side and studied me through narrowed eyes. "Sure, if you look at it that way. But there is plenty you can do about it."

"Huh? You just said—"

"Hey"—he did this geeky multiple finger snapping thing, like he was the hip but aging host of some *American Bandstand* kind of show, or something—"your old dad can put a positive spin on anything. You know that."

"Go for it, spin doctor," I challenged, arching one brow.

He swiveled his tall stool toward me. "Captaining a ship," he began in a grand voice, "is a whole lot like life."

"Whoo-boy, here we go." I crossed my arms.

He held up a palm. "Just listen. As long as you set a course, keep your ultimate destination in mind, and your eyes and radar pointed in that direction, it's okay to drift off-course now and then. It's all about misstep and correction. Over and over. That, my dear, is life."

"Whatever. That's weird."

He shrugged, as if my assessment was up for debate. "I don't know. Maybe life is weird, and the ship is just a metaphor for it. Ever think of that?"

I shook my head. Yeah, because I always sit around thinking up pithy metaphors to explain why my life blows. Have a clue much, Pops?

"You just do your best, keep the goal in mind, and head

on out. No path is perfect, and we're all in the same boat, so to speak." He laughed at his own not-that-funny pun.

I pulled my feet up to sit cross-legged while simultaneously stretching my dress over my knees. "Easy for you to laugh about it. Your path was perfect," I said. "You wanted to be a ship captain, you found out what it would take, did it, and voilà—you're here. It was cake for you."

Dad's eyes opened a touch wider, and his mouth spread into a puzzled smile. "Is that really how you think it happened for me?"

"Didn't it?"

"No, Camille. Not even close. Sure, I wanted to be a ship's captain, just like other guys wanted to be astronauts or pro ballplayers or the president. But I doubted myself and my abilities like any other young person with a dream."

"Sure you did," I said with scorn.

He nodded. "It's true. I changed my mind so many times about what I wanted to do, your *abuelita* almost gave up on me."

"Grams wouldn't do that."

"No. Not really. But I exasperated her."

"Yeah, I feel her pain," I teased.

He shook his fist at me playfully. "I almost became a priest, you know."

I pulled my chin back and bugged my eyes. "You?"

"Don't act so surprised."

I swung my arms wide. "Surprised? More like horrified."

"Why?"

"What daughter wouldn't freak at the thought of her *father* almost becoming a priest? News flash: celibacy? One small twist of fate, and I wouldn't even *be* here. That's creepy." I made a face. "Plus, there's the whole long robe, kiss my ring ick-factor."

Dad bit back a laugh he probably wished I hadn't seen, then aimed his pointer finger at me. "Don't you ever say that 'long robe, kiss my ring' stuff around your grandmother, *M'ija*. It's sacrilegious. She'll have us all doing rosaries until we're hoarse."

"Whatever, Dad." I gave him a knowing smile. "You're so not priestly. And that comment is just further proof."

"Believe me, I know." He lifted his shiny-billed captain hat off, smoothed his hair, then settled the hat back on his head. "But the point is, it took me jumping off my course and back on repeatedly before I figured out who I really was."

"A ship's captain?"

"A ship's captain who finally knew he could do it." He pinned me with a soft look. "And that's okay. Years from now, this SAT stuff?" He whistled through his teeth while aiming one thumb over his shoulder. "You won't even remember it. Trust me."

"Riiiiiight." I crossed my arms, turned my head, and gave him a look out of the corner of my eye. "Does that mean I can save time and blow it off now?"

He glared.

"Just kidding."

"Of course you are."

"So . . . come clean with me, Pops."

"Yeah?"

"This whole conversation has been one of those touchy-feely teaching moments, hasn't it?"

A knock sounded on the door. Cheeseburger delivery, no doubt, and just in the nick of time.

"You," he growled, grabbing me around the neck for a soft noogie as he headed across the room to open the door. "I'll take my unexpected teaching moments wherever and whenever I can find them, kiddo."

www.NobodyGetsJiggy.com

So, I accidentally on purpose got shitfaced with L last night. It was SOOOO fun and worth it, even though I promised C's dad I wouldn't drink this summer. But, COME ON . . . does he really think we won't? It's SUPER easy to sneak down to the crew deck, and even though Camille's and my cards are "flagged" to show we're underage, it's a snap to get a drink. Or several!

We had to go the total stealth route to smuggle me back to my room without getting busted by (1) C's dad; or (2) someone who would run off and report me to C's dad. Not only would I be in trouble if that happened, but C and L would probably catch a little of that backlash too. I don't want that. Can you imagine if I got L fired, after all she's been through?!?!

Anyway, C was CRASHED OUT when I got back, and I didn't wake her. I'm pretty sure she doesn't know I was trashed, not that I'm trying to keep it from her, necessarily. I just don't want to put her in the position of having to lie to her dad so early in the summer.

I must say, however, that it SO completely sucked getting up for work this morning. But with a whole bunch of concealer, water, aspirin, Pepto Bismol, and buckets of the free coffee I get at work, I am surviving. Only one hour left before I can collapse in a deck chair somewhere. I followed L's advice and ate a plain double cheeseburger for lunch. She claims they have magical hangover curing properties, and while I'm not so sure of the MAGIC aspect, at least my stomach has settled.

Okay, so I've chosen my new summer motto: On a cruise ship, you only have to fall in love with them for a week at a time. LOL!!!! I admit it, I got it from L. It's really *her* motto, but I'm going to adopt it. I mean, as employees, we're not *technically* allowed to hook up with passengers, but SHIT HAPPENS. I figure, I'm not a real employee, anyway. Plus, L hooks up with passengers all the time and never gets caught. (She so rules. I swear. She's my idol.) Besides, I'm not looking for a BOYFRIEND this summer. That's so horkingly TYPICAL, and I refuse to go back to Madison trapped into some long-distance romance that will completely cramp my style (the style I hope to acquire while here, that is). Please. It's going to be my senior year! All I'm looking for over the next three months is a little quality time with my inner party girl . . . and whoever is lucky enough to be invited to her party.

On that note, the big announcement is . . .

::::Drumroll Please::::

I've decided I will no longer wait to LOSE my virginity, which is such a negative way to phrase it. LOSING IT. As if you're not paying attention and—OOPS—it falls out of your purse on the subway or something, only to be trampled alongside the gum wrappers and losing lotto tickets by a million oblivious commuters. Instead, I choose to be proactive and empowered and GIVE mine away. Exactly when, and to whom, is yet to be determined. But the where (on the ship) and the why (why not?) are all worked out. This is the perfect place to orchestrate my own memorable FIRST TIME, which might sound a little overplanned and clinical. But, even if you do wait for that One Special Guy and the Lifelong True Commitment and the Perfect Spontaneous Moment, it can all backfire, like it did for L. And like it could've for C, which would've been the WORST—losing it with B.

It's not worth leaving it to fate or placing so much importance on it that your life suddenly SUCKS when the so-called love goes away. I'll take the planned fantasy any day, and what could be more exciting and memorable than hooking up on a ship with some hot stranger who you'll never see again, except in your dreams?

I've just decided that it doesn't have to be this huge, ceremonial MILESTONE in my life. I prefer to think of it as more of a resurfacing of my life path. Who needs stupid speed bumps to slow you down? Caution is overrated. I'm pedal to the metal from here on out.

So, here are the four simple rules for my Inner Party Girl Virginity Eradication Program:

1. No crew members, because that would be weird and would come with baggage or commitment, or something else equally restraining and icky. And it doesn't matter if I know him well or not, anyway. As L says, whether it's a drive-thru or a sit-down gourmet meal, you're still eating.

2. No emotional attachment. I'll keep the power with me, thank you.

3. I can choose to keep in touch or not afterward, but it's up to me. And if I choose TO, it's strictly a friendship thing. I WILL NOT BE IN LOVE WITH MY LUCKY VIRGINITY RECIPIENT. That way, the memory can never be tainted by heartbreak.

4. Maximum of a three-night-stand, otherwise it gets too relationshipy feeling.

I'm all for getting it the hell over with on MY

terms. Plus, it will make me feel somewhat vindicated if I have that little secret side my parentals know nothing about. Let them believe I'm perfect, if that's what they need to get them through the day. But I will NOT head off to college as Little Miss Obedient Daughter Who Always Does Everything RIGHT. That's gotten me NOWHERE fast. By the time I move into the dorms, I plan to be worldly, wild, well traveled, and willing—unafraid of a little casual sex, if it serves my purposes. Think about it: The less sacred we make the whole first-time sex thing, the more power we (women) have over getting hurt or burned.

Wow, I'm almost sounding like C. <scary> Except she's keeping her power by ABSTAINING, while I want to keep mine by ENTERTAINING.

Who luvs ya, baby?

The Goddess of NobodyGetsJiggy(.com)

P.S. Can't believe I almost forgot this!! L and I have SO TOTALLY come up with the perfect revenge plot against B, on behalf of C. If I have anything to say about it, his senior year is going to S-U-U-UCK the big red hooter. I'm not going to tell C until it's all underway. It will be my special gift for her!

chapter eight

I survived the first two weeks of my three-month job sentence (without possibility of parole) by doing everything within my supremely limited power to steer clear of Makaio during our daily four-hour shared "lockdown." I know—sounds simple enough, right? Well, it wasn't, considering he's my JOB MENTOR (DUH!) and, hence, he's supposed to MENTOR me through this so-called rollicking good time known in my mind as The Summer of a Thousand Traumas.

Each morning, I politely volunteered for every craptastic crop of grunt work that came along, no matter how vile, just so I wouldn't be forced into close proximity with Makaio. I seriously could not handle watching as he dazzled the new rock-wall climbers with his skills, encouragement, and big sense of hang-loose, island fun.

Here's the cool thing about guys, though: They just don't GET IT most of the time. Case in point, Makaio had no clue I was volunteering for the shit jobs to avoid him. He just thought I was a super-great worker, always willing to take one for the team. HOOO-RAH!

As if.

I wasn't sure I could survive this for the whole summer, especially considering the fact that, despite my best efforts to the contrary, I'd fallen victim to my own traitorous hormones. I couldn't seem to shake this super-annoying über-awareness of Makaio that had overtaken my brain. For 240 minutes of each workday while I "avoided" him, every cell in my body was entirely tuned in to his every move, and man, I gotta tell you, the whole situation was just beating me down. He was fun, funny, easygoing. Oh, and HOT.

Freakin' scorching hot.

Like, *melt-away-all-a-girl's-resistance-and-self-esteem* hot.

And yet he didn't seem aware of it like Brett the Barftastic always was (which should've been a clue!).

I know . . . you're thinking cruise ship, hot Hawaiian guy, four-hour workdays . . . CRY ME A RIVER, CAMILLE. But look at it from my perspective: I wasn't even partially on the way to recovery from having been "Brettacked," and now I was totally trapped in the middle of the ocean with the hottest guy in the HISTORY of hot guys, in the WHOLE DAMN UNIVERSE.

Don't get me wrong—he treated me just like a pal. No flirting whatsoever. But whenever part of the fitness deck crew got together after their work hours, he always invited me. Luckily, he always accepted it easily when I begged off, too. No pressure. But, the worst part—seriously—was how nice he treated me.

I had to remind myself (repeatedly) that Brett had treated me well, too—initially. Whatever. I didn't trust myself enough to know whether Makaio was REALLY a good guy or if he was just PLAYING the good-guy role while operating with an underlying agenda, and the bottom line was, I DIDN'T WANT TO THINK ABOUT THIS SHIT ALL SUMMER LONG!

Bitter, party of one? Your job is ready.

Hence, my avoidance plan, which was only half-assedly working, because Makaio, like I said, had become an occupying force in my brainscape.

On that third Wednesday—the first day of several scheduled "family cruise weeks"—we set sail from Oahu beneath perfect turquoise skies. Our fresh batch of cruisers included a much larger than usual percentage of kids and teens, which Jiggy and I were counting on to provide a nice change of pace. That morning, just like every morning, I walked Jiggy to Vibe, snagged myself a skinny soy latte with an extra shot, then made my way to the fitness deck for my scheduled four hours. I was full-on planning to make my usual getaway into menial chore oblivion, but—

"Camille," Makaio said, the moment I arrived in our work area. He wore the standard fitness crew garb: fitted sky blue polo shirt with the cruise line's insignia embroidered on the left chest area and MAKAIO on the right, along with black climbing pants—cruel to look at, let me tell you. I wore a similar getup, but my polo was embroidered with the word INTERN, and I didn't have a name. Anyway, he beckoned me over to the wall with one hand, seemingly unaware of how his mere presence was obliterating my personal growth.

"What's up?" I asked, trying unsuccessfully to mask my decided lack of enthusiasm. I checked my watch to make sure I wasn't late and, hence, due for a smackdown.

He smiled. "I'm really sorry, but I need you to belay with me today, yah?"

"Oh." That's it? "Okay." Despite my reluctance to be that close to him for four straight hours, I actually felt my spirits rise. Climbing was the most fun, but belaying could be entertaining too. In any case, it beat picking up sweaty, nasty old discarded towels. YECH! "But, why are you sorry?"

"I wasn't sure you were into the climbing wall."

Heh? "Whatever gave you that idea?" I set my coffee on a nearby table next to a teak deck chair, leaned my shoulder down to slide my hot pink duffel onto the chaise, then pulled my hair into a ponytail with the black elastic I'd slipped over my wrist as I left the stateroom.

He shrugged. "You always volunteer for other jobs. And you haven't climbed yet. Have you?"

"Oh. Well . . . no. I mean, not yet. But I love the wall."

"Works out great, then."

Glancing around uneasily, I asked, "Where's Faustino?" Our geeky but endearingly cheerful Spanish coworker generally (thank God) worked the wall with Makaio during my shift.

"Belowdecks." Makaio grimaced. "He got a wicked case of food poisoning last night when he was on shore leave."

"That blows." I flipped my hand over and scrunched up my nose. "I mean . . . no pun intended. Ew."

One corner of his mouth lifted. "Yeah, no way he could belay with having to run to the john every five seconds, know what I'm sayin'?."

I nodded. Uh, yeah. Not much mystery there.

"So Doc told him to take the day off and rest."

"I suppose it would be smart to find out where he ate so we can avoid it." Stupid small talk. BLEH, it sucked. I stepped in to help Makaio stack rope in preparation for the long and undoubtedly *painful* day ahead.

He hiked his chin toward my drink. "Go 'head and finish your coffee while I do this. We're gonna be swamped when the crowd gets here, *garans*, and there won't be too many breaks."

"Okay. Thanks."

"Guess I should ask. You know how to belay, yah?"

"Of course," I said, trying not to feel indignant. I returned to the deck chair, shoved my duffel out of the way, and sat. "I went through training and certification at our local climbing gym in Madison more than a year ago."

"I thought that's what I'd been told, but like I said"—he hiked one shoulder apologetically—"I jus' hadn't seen you going for it. So I asked."

"Well, I've been running a lot." Why did I say that?

What an idiot. Like I had to prove to the guy I was athletic or something? Gag. "There's only so much time, I guess. I have to study a lot this summer."

"Study for what?"

"The SAT. *Makeup* SAT, that is. It's a long, ugly story." I waved away any further questions. "But don't worry, I can belay. I love to belay." He didn't press me on the SAT stuff, and I liked that he didn't.

"So, we'll work alongside each other, yah? Maybe you can stay an extra couple of hours if it gets all *pupule* round here. Crazy," he added, at my look of confusion. I was catching on to some of his Hawaiian slang, but that was a new one on me.

"Oh. Sure." Kill me now. I slipped my sunglasses on, mostly to hide my eyes.

"Awesome. I owe you for that."

"No, it's okay. You don't," I said, more firmly than I'd intended. I didn't want him to feel indebted, though.

"Your call." He organized the harnesses and sorted the shoes into large bamboo baskets by size, so the cruisers could easily find them. Squinting up at me in the sun, he said, "The teen cruise directors are escorting a huge group up this morning for lessons. Then another this afternoon."

"Is it always this way during family cruise weeks?"

"You mean, with all the kids? Big groups?"

I nodded.

"Yep. *Uku* plenty climbers." He systematically checked all the air traffic controller belay devices while I systematically avoided looking at his ripped biceps. "You handle the smaller kids. I'll take the big guys and the adults. We'll figure out a system."

"Whatever works." For some inexplicable reason, I started to relax. I took a sip of my coffee, then visually traced the various color-tagged climbing routes up the impressive, multistory wall. My gaze moved from bucket to chimney to chickenhead as I planned out which ones I'd grab and step on as I worked my way to the summit. Some of the routes looked way challenging, which would be totally fun. They'd even designed a couple of roofs into the wall for the more experienced climbers. At the very top stood a sign: E MAKAUKAU `OE ME KA MANA `O WIWO `OLE, and just below it, the translation in English: GET READY WITHOUT FEAR.

I did want to climb the thing, Makaio or not. Boy, did I.

"Do we allow bouldering?" I asked, suddenly. The gym at home had rules about how high climbers could go without safety restraints, but below that, the wall was fair game.

"Not here." He hiked his chin to indicate the vast body of water upon which we floated. "Sometimes you can't tell when the ship's going to roll. It's not worth the risk. Nobody goes on this wall unsecured, that's rule number one."

I considered that, glanced around for any spies, then lowered my voice. "Yeah, but do you guys ever free solo when the wall's closed to passengers?"

Makaio cocked his head to one side, the gleam in his eye saying he was impressed. "Well, now. Camille Tafoya is a danger junkie. You learn something new every day."

"Oh, be quiet." I couldn't quite hide my smile.

"Does Captain Dad know you walk on the wild side?"

I challenged him with a raised eyebrow. "Is that a no to my question?"

He smirked and sort of shook his head. "It's a no. We don't take any unnecessary risks on the ship. It's just not worth it with the liability issues, and most of want to keep our jobs, yah?"

Made sense. "Bummer, though."

He conceded with a shrug. "Anyway, the exciting climbs are on the islands, not on the ship. You oughtta come with us on shore leave next time we're on my island."

His island, I knew from two straight weeks of obsessive eavesdropping, was the Big Island: Hawaii.

"I can take you to some awesome places, Camille. Hi'ilawe Falls in the Waipi'o Valley?" He shook his head, a dreamy look on his face. "It's beautiful, yah? You can jump right into the falls. *Buckaloose*, yah? Just out of control."

"For real?"

"Well . . . I'm not sure we're technically supposed to jump, but you can. If you're not afraid, that is."

Afraid. SCOFF. As if. "That sounds totally cool."

He laughed softly. "It is. Just say the word, and you're welcome to come along. As long as your dad won't kill me for risking your life and limb."

Like Makaio would be all responsible for me and stuff. GLUG! Set myself up for that one. "Oh. Well. I'll uh . . .

think about it," I murmured, knowing I SO TOTALLY WOULDN'T. The last thing I needed was to spend my off-duty time with the guy too.

"So she *is* afraid of something," he joked.

"I am *so* not afraid. That's not it."

"What is it, then?"

"I'm just busy."

"Uh-huh. Sure." He winked.

I scowled.

For a few moments, Makaio worked in easy silence, and I watched from the deck chair, my Vibe cup in hand.

"So, are you finding any time to have fun while you're here, even though you have to study?" he asked without looking up. "I've seen Jiggy a couple times at the Tonga Club on Maui with Lani Katsura, but never you."

The Tonga Club. I'd never even heard of the place. Well, that wasn't *exactly* true. I mean, Jiggy had talked about all the different clubs they'd been to, but none of them stuck in my head. I felt so out of the loop, and even though I'd *chosen* not to go with them, a pang of envy contracted my gut.

"Oh. Well." What could I say? I'm not much of a club person? I don't feel like hitting the Polynesian party scene? I'm not into hunting for boys? I'm a total dork? "I just . . . haven't gone. I don't know." Yeah, that answer sucked. Whatever.

"You're not missing much. A club scene is a club scene, *`aole anei?*" He shrugged, blasé.

Like I knew. "Uh, yeah. What did you just say?"

He looked up, confused for a moment, then he shook his head. "Sorry. Means, 'isn't that so?'" He smiled. "Hard to break, the language habit. I get better about it as the summer goes on, though."

I nodded, used to hearing someone throw random foreign phrases into a conversation, because my dad and my grandma both did it all the time with Spanish. But I understood most of theirs, whereas his meant zippola to me.

"But, really, if you aren't afraid—"

"I'm *not*."

"Good. Come with us next time. Now, that waterfall's an unforgettable scene."

Kind of like the one I was staring at now . . . Makaio, muscles flexing through his fitted T-shirt as he worked. I tore my gaze away. "Who's us?" I asked, suddenly curious, and grateful to be off the topic of the heretofore unexplored (by me, that is) club scene.

"A group from the fitness deck. Faustino, me. A couple of the other guys. Some of my friends from home."

Um, yeah. Not even.

A bunch of guys + Camille Tafoya = disaster.

We'd worked that equation before, folks!

"Well? Ms. 'No Fear' poster child, you'll come along?"

I hesitated. Oh. He expected an actual answer?

"Imagine the bragging rights you'll have when you get back to your indoor gym."

"I told you, I'll think about it."

"That's a no."

I rolled my eyes. "It's a *maybe*."

"It's pure fear, or you'd give me a yes." He crossed his arms, looking smug. "Any climber would jump at that chance."

I made a face. "You don't know what you're talking about."

"Say yes. C'mon, Camille. I dare you."

I started to tell him what to do with his dare, but a crowd of kids and teens barreled around the corner, chattering and laughing, along with two teen cruise directors I recognized from the Meet & Greets. "Duty calls," I said, flashing him a nanner-nanner smile before draining the last of my java and evading his stupid dare.

"Chicken," he muttered under his breath.

"I am *not*."

"What are you, then?"

I opened my mouth, then closed it and shook my head, deciding not to take the bait.

"Thought so," he teased, then added, *"Ho'o Mau!"* with a hang loose gesture of one hand.

"Say what?"

"It means 'climb on' in Hawaiian. That one, you've gotta learn." He grinned, then stood to welcome the group.

As expected, all the girls appeared immediately starstruck or recently lobotomized, I wasn't sure which. They stood before Makaio, slackjawed and/or preening, staring as if he'd just sprung from the pages of a romance novel to rescue them from their regular, boring-ass lives.

I sucked in a long, slow breath, then eased it out on a ten count, reminding myself I was no better than any of them. No smarter. Reminding myself rather harshly that this was why I'd wound up here, why my summer goal was to learn from my own humiliating mistakes. And anything involving Makaio—even climbing a rock wall and jumping off into a waterfall, fun and surreal as that sounds—would be a HUGE mistake. Even if I did it only to prove I wasn't afraid. Because I *was* afraid.

Very.

Just . . . not of the waterfall.

DING! . . . Let the nausea begin.

chapter nine

The rest of that first month and week one of the second zipped by as Jiggy and I adapted to our new lives, albeit using vastly different methods. Of course, we still hung out, sunbathing and eating and shopping together almost every day. We walked to work together each morning, and shared stories about our jobs LONG after we should've already been asleep. But beyond that, we'd split off in different directions, mostly because *I* didn't feel like going out, and *Jigs* didn't feel like staying in.

Which worked fine for both of us.

I'd fallen into a comfortably divided routine of working, running, and studying, while Jiggy's consisted mostly of partying, piercing, and flirting. Okay, not fair. She spent a ton of time at Vibe, working more hours than she had to, just because she loved it. Everyone there seemed to respect her talents and her work ethic.

As for me, after Faustino's food poisoning day, my apprehension about working with Makaio waned a bit, although I can't really explain why. I just welcomed the new comfort level. Faustino and I took turns belaying with Makaio, or sometimes all three of us worked the wall when things got crazy. Makaio and I had slipped into this casually fun teasing pattern that somehow made me feel safer around him. You know . . . he repeatedly accused me of being too scared to climb the waterfall, I struck back with whatever excellent barbs I could concoct on the spur of the moment. Faustino joined in, too, and that upped the chill factor even more.

They kept politely inviting me to join in on crew parties.

I kept politely refusing.

Everything seemed to be going well, considering.

Jiggy, meanwhile, was having the time of her life, and I loved hearing about her exploits—although some of them worried me a tad. With each passing day, she grew a little bolder about breaking the rules my dad had laid down. Oh yeah, that was another large component of my life now: covering for Jiggy—not that I minded. What's a best friend for? Plus, a lot of that was my fault, what with me being the one who'd encouraged her to forget her parents and live it up this summer. I just never expected the pendulum to swing so far to the wild side, prompting her to engage in such un-Jiggy-esque behavior as (1) sneaking around and getting plowed—on a regular basis—with a much older crowd; (2) launching an all-out hunt for the perfect unimportant guy to SLEEP WITH, of all things, and; (3) piercing a new body part every time she could get off the ship long enough to visit a piercing parlor. So far, that included left eyebrow, nose, right nipple, and belly button.

Okay, I dug the piercings (except for the nipple, which made me wince just thinking about it), but I also knew Jiggy's parents, and I can't say I didn't worry about how THEY might react to all the "redecorating." My dad seemed okay with the eyebrow after Jiggy somehow managed to convince him the nose jewel was a stick on. (Clueless) He didn't know about the other two, thank God.

Anyway, fooling my dad was one thing, but her own parents? I mean, what if they freaked out and blamed *my* dad for . . . I don't know . . . not supervising us closely enough? What if a big war ensued, after which they decided Jiggy and I couldn't hang out anymore? I know it's self-centered, but can you even grasp how much my senior year would suck?

And then there were the guys.

Many, many, MANY guys.

Jiggy hadn't found *The Right Guy* for her weird summer sex plan yet, but she sure was taking a lot of test-drives, if you catch my drift. I mean, hey, it's all good. I'm down with trying on shoes before you commit to wearing them long-term. But her cold, calculating determination to fulfill this goal was what concerned me. The Jiggy back home just didn't *DO* that, ya know? What had prompted it?

Each week, a new crop of possibilities boarded the ship, and, I swear, she scrutinized them as if she were choosing dinner from a menu. *Chicken? No, I had that for lunch. I think I'll go for the big, juicy T-bone this time.* I'm not even exaggerating. I started to think maybe I should suck it up and go out with her and Lani every now and then, if only to keep an eye on my newly judgment-impaired best friend.

As if I were the queen of good judgment. Ha.

The simple fact that I felt mine might be more sound than hers should give you a clue as to how *much* Jiggy had changed. In light of that, nothing should've surprised me, right?

So, the second week of our second month, Jiggy and I were taking advantage of the fact that most of the passengers had gotten off the ship to explore Maui by chilling in the nearly empty spa, which had become a twice-a-week habit for us. We were covered neck to feet in antioxidant mud baths, reclined on a couple of plastic chaises. As we sat in the warm room drying, Jiggy suddenly said, "Oh, yeah."

She stood, reached into the pocket of her beach cover-up, which she'd hung on a nearby wall hook, extracted some folded papers, and then passed them to me without a word.

I glanced from them, back to her, as she settled into her chair again. "What's this?"

"Read it."

So I did.

Once, and then again. Holy—

"What in the HELL *is* this, Jiggy?" The dirt-smeared papers crinkled in my hands as I lowered them to my super grimy lap. "Where did you get it?"

She grinned at me. "I wrote it."

"You—" I stared at it again, my eyes jumping to phrases such as *whacks off compulsively* and *wears girls' underwear* and *teenage bedwetter*. If she wrote it, it had to be—

"Wait a minute." I gaped at her in disbelief. The fact that Jiggy had grown wilder over the weeks was crystal clear, but I'd missed the part where she'd jumped the fence into flat-out NUTSO. Where the hell had I been? Stuck inside an SAT prep book? Preoccupied with convincing Makaio I wasn't afraid of the damned waterfall climb? Preoccupied with Makaio, period? "This is your blog? Your *baby*? I didn't even know you were posting to it this summer, especially not stuff like . . . this."

"Oh, well." Jiggy's gaze cut away, and she cleared her throat. "It's not my blog."

Relief. "Phew. Then what—?"

"You told me to ask Lani for good revenge ideas that first night I went partying with her, remember?"

"I was kidding."

"Still, it was a great idea, whether you meant it or not. So, I did. Ask her, I mean. Anyway, we came up with this." She pointed toward the papers still death-clutched in my lap. "It's a new blog I'm writing. Anonymously, so don't worry about my regular blog rep. It's safe and sound."

"Good . . . I think."

"So, anyway, it's called, TheTruthAboutBrett.com."

Truth? "And you know for a fact that Brett Mason wears girls' underwear?"

"Well," she said, her face tilted at a sly angle, "he lied about you. Paybacks are a bitch."

As much as I wished I could take the higher road, I simply couldn't argue her point.

"I've opened the blog up for other people's entries, too, real or fake. It's sort of like a blogboard."

I shook my head, half smiling. "More like a blog *bash*."

"Exactly. And the jerk deserves it. How much do you want to bet you weren't the first girl he treated poorly?"

I blinked, absorbing her train of thought. "You think other 'victims' will come out of the woodwork and add their own stories after reading this?"

She flashed a smug smile my way and crossed her fingers, muddy hands held high. "But, until that happens, I'll be adding more. Under aliases, of course. And Lani's working on a new entry tonight, too. Don't you love it?"

Okay, I admit it was funny, in a wrong-on-so-many-levels kind of way. Jiggy had made Brett Mason out to be the biggest cheat, liar, and nose-picking sexual deviant you could ever imagine. She'd held NOTHING back—including his full name, address, phone number, school, birthdate, and e-mail addy—which had to break some kind of law, I was sure.

Of course, he'd probably never see it, which was fine. It was still cathartic to read. "I can't believe you did this." I covered my smile with the muddy back of my hand. "It's . . ."

"Awesome?" Jigs asked.

It was. It really was. But it also made me nervous for a lot of reasons I couldn't quite pinpoint. "Well, it *is* hilarious. And he deserves it, for sure." I reread a few lines, snickering. "It would be cool if all the popular people who think they know the real him could read it. Girls, especially." But, then again, that might lead to uncomfy questions . . . or back to Jiggy. "Maybe not."

"That," Jiggy said in a matter-of-fact tone, "has been taken care of." She pulled a Tinkerbell compact mirror out of the plastic tote bag she'd set next to her chair and examined her pearlescent lip gloss as though she were dressed for a date rather than covered in slimy brown mud.

My nerves zinged with warning. "Meaning what?"

"Meaning, Lani helped me hack into the Midwest Academy server and spam the entire school with it. Except the faculty, of course." She snapped the compact shut. "And we're tracking it. So far, ninety MA students have at least opened the e-mail containing the blog link and invitation. Once they realize it's about one of their tarnished golden boys, you *know* they'll read it." She held up a finger. "*And* talk about it, which is the key. It'll be all over Wisconsin before you can say cheese curd."

My heart hammered in my ears as I stared at her with utter disbelief. On the one hand, SO COOL. But on the other hand . . . "Jiggy," I said, in as level a tone as I could manage, what with the panic rising like a dancing cobra in my chest.

"Yeah?" She held her arms out in front of her, studying the cracking mud near her elbows. She didn't appear the least bit concerned.

"Jane Goodall Yearling," I said, more sternly.

"Hey!" She frowned, glancing around to make sure no one had heard her real name. Not that anyone else was in mudland with us, but she was determined to keep it under wraps this summer. "You promised not to call me that."

"Stick to the subject." I waved a hand in front of her face. "You *do* realize you used the verbs 'hack' and 'spam' in one sentence about yourself without even blinking, don't you?"

She paused, considering this, then shrugged. "Yeah, so? We're going to try to crack the public schools in Madison, too. I'm sure Brett gets around."

My vision wavered. "No, Jigs! You can't!"

"He deserves it. You said it yourself."

"Well, yeah. You could argue that he deserves to be run over by a bus, too, but that doesn't mean it's legal to do so."

"Oh, legal." She waved it away. "*That's* what you're wigging about?"

Who are you, and what have you done with my sane, rule-following, "good influence" best friend? "Um . . . YEAH. What else? Suppose you get busted?"

"I'm not worried about it."

I huffed. "Well, great. That makes one of us."

"Why are you stressing?" A line of annoyance marred her suntanned forehead. "This was supposed to be a nice surprise for you."

"It was. But the hacking part—"

"You told me to have fun this summer. Plus, I knew you'd be too nice to seek revenge against Brett, so I'm doing it for you. That's what friends are for. No need to thank me."

I sat forward, lowering my voice to an urgent rasp. "Jigs, I appreciate your creativity. I do. The blog is freakin' hilarious. But, you've crossed a line. You're a HACKER." I paused, letting that sink in. "Hacking is ILLEGAL. *Comprende?* Do you really want to go to prison and be Big Bertha's bee-yatch?"

"Not likely."

"But possible. Are you willing to risk it?"

"For you? Of course."

Incredulous, I shook my head. "Jigs. Seriously. You're the best friend ever. But seeking revenge against Brett is not worth getting in trouble over. And I don't want you to go to prison on my behalf."

She laughed. "Lighten up, Sister Mary DoGooder. It's not like I'm sending out a worm virus. I'm just giving a WORM exactly what he deserves. Small potatoes. It's all good."

I scrambled out of my muddy seat and loomed before her, fists on my hips. Was I the only one seeing the BIG PICTURE here?! "Yeah, it's all good until *someone* gets expelled from Midwest Academy just before our senior year, leaving me to wallow in the suckdom of that hellhole all by myself."

"Camille," she said, in an excessively patient tone. "Darling. I am *not* going to get expelled. I'm not even going to get caught." She crossed one brown leg over the other, the dried mud on her knee breaking into wavy lines as she bent it. "I'm going to ease in, destroy Brett's life, and then ease out before anyone knows what hit them. Trust me."

It struck me that she sounded more like Lani with each passing day—a sobering thought. Even though I got along really well with Lani and I knew Jiggy adored her, I wasn't sure what I felt about Jiggy morphing into her clone. Lani's wild streak bordered on reckless, and as much as I'd wanted Jiggy to sever her parental approval reins, her hero-worship of Lani had begun to scare me. *Not* because I was jealous, either—that wasn't it. Jiggy's and my friendship was rock solid. Without sounding like a mother hen (hopefully), I just worried about the direction she'd been heading lately.

But I couldn't continue to nag her or she'd end up hating me. I started to pace, and the drying mud made my skin itch. "Oh, my God," I murmured, mostly to myself.

She sighed. "Can you just let me do this, Cam? It's making me feel a whole lot better to actually *do* something."

"Something like retaliate?"

"So? It's hurting no one, except Brett, and the bastard earned it."

God, had he ever. I paused, my back to her, and bit the

corner of my bottom lip. I tried to remember all the sayings I'd ever heard about revenge backfiring, but none of them came to mind. I mean, if she was *enjoying* herself . . . because I did screw up her entire summer, after all. Plus, she knew more about computer stuff than I did—by far. Maybe the getting busted thing really was a long shot, and I was freaking out for nothing. Maybe the blog *was* all in good fun.

I spun to face her, leveling her with a narrowed, serious gaze. "Okay, fine. Blog away, but on one condition."

"Name it."

"You have to promise me you'll stop if I ask you to. I mean, this is *my* battle to fight. Or not. If I decide to let it go, you have to respect that, whether you think I'm being weak and passive or not."

We locked gazes, and several strained moments passed.

"Deal," Jiggy said, finally. She leaned off her chaise, scooped a handful of mud from the floor, and pitched it directly into my face. "Chickenshit," she said with a wink that told me we were okay again.

I stood there stunned for a minute, before emitting a squeal of playful outrage. "Mudslinging ho," I said, smearing it off my forehead and chucking it back at her. "And I mean that in more ways than one!"

"Them's fightin' words," she said, lunging down behind her chaise to pack a new ball.

I scraped up a mud missle of my own and let it fly. "Stop hiding behind that chair if you're going to accuse *me* of being chicken!"

A raucous mudfight ensued until the tension had dissipated and we were breathless with laughter. We stood across the room from each other, spitting out globs of the gritty stuff and shaking clumps of it from our hair. Each one hit the floor with a nasty sounding splat.

The spa lady stuck her head in the mudbath room and raised her eyebrows. "You're dry enough. Time to rinse, young ladies," she said, in the pretty East Indian accent that just barely hid her exasperation with our antics.

"Yes, ma'am," we said in unison.

"It's been very refreshing," Jiggy added, in her carefully honed, adult-pleasing voice.

"I can see that. Go on now." The spa lady's rueful tone let us know she didn't buy the goody-two-shoes act at all. We both knew she was cutting us slack because I was the captain's daughter. But, that wasn't cool. We needed to straighten up before we got banned from the spa facilities for the rest of the summer.

"Come on." I tugged Jiggy's arm, heading for the warm showers near the back of the room. "I need to study, anyway. Ugh."

"Study, schmuddy," Jiggy said, grabbing my shoulder to stop me. "It's our day off, and Maui is *right there*." She pointed out the big windows toward the lush island where we'd docked earlier that day. "You have yet to leave the ship and explore this island, and it rocks."

"What do you have in mind?" I didn't really feel like studying, anyway. I reached into one of the stalls and twisted the faucet. The pipes squealed briefly, and then a massaging spray of water shot out. I held my hand under to test the temperature, stepping in when it was steamy.

Jiggy did the same in her stall. "Let's go drinking with Lani."

"What?"

"Come on. She's off, too, and there's a great club in Lahaina that's always packed with hot guys—not that you care," she added in a rush, before I could squawk. "But, I do. I still haven't found *him*." Meaningful pause. "And I've been there before. They won't card us."

I ignored the reference to Jiggy's hunt for her Virginity Eradication Program guy, because, even though I understood her rationale, I wasn't sure how I felt about the whole thing. I was glad she enjoyed being the giant flirt-monster, but still.

"I don't know, Jigs." I'd managed to stay out of trouble so far, and—I admit it—I liked the fact that my dad was starting to trust me more. "I can't just *go drinking*." I peeled off my dirty bikini, then scrubbed, watching the chocolatey rivulets of mud trickle down my body and swirl into the drain. "What about my dad?"

She raised her voice to be heard over the WHOOSH of our two side-by-side showers. "What about him? I've gotten away with it. Numerous times."

"Thanks to my cover." I tipped my face into the spray.

"Only that once. And I was fine hiding under the table in the crew lounge. I could've stayed there for hours."

It *wasn't* just that once. I rolled my eyes, then unwrapped a bar of fresh plumeria soap and started to suds up. "Still."

"Well, then drink Diet Pepsi, if it makes you more comfortable. But come with us. Please?" Her face appeared around the corner of my stall. "Pretty please with chocolate on top?"

I rinsed.

And rinsed.

And rinsed some more.

"Okay, fine, I'll go," I said casually.

"What?" she shrieked, busting into a huge smile. "Really?"

I shrugged, as though it meant nothing to me, but inside, it felt great to see her excitement. Heck, with all the practice I had at my job, I could snub guys for a few hours if it meant making my best friend happy. I mean, hell, she'd branded Brett Mason a *teddy bear humper* over the INTERNET. For that slam, if nothing else, I owed her BIG-TIME. "Finish showering so we can get ready before I change my mind," I said, with feigned sternness.

Jiggy cheered as she ducked back into her own stall. "You won't regret it, Camille! I promise."

Yeah . . . sure I wouldn't.

Why is it whenever anyone utters those words, the opposite always seems to come true?

www.NobodyGetsJiggy.com

Super-quick check-in, boyz 'n' grrrrrrlz. I have to run back to my room and finish getting my sexy on, but I HAD to share. DIG IT: C's FINALLY going out with me and L tonight!! CIRCLE THIS DAY ON YOUR CALENDARS, because that is the mark of something special. I can't wait to introduce her to the club and show her what she's been missing all summer. Maybe I'll find the perfect you-know-what guy at the club. C always has been my good luck charm, bringing me just what I need, just when I need it. I can't see why it would be any different now!

I don't know, but I just have this sense that something big's going to happen tonight. I can feel the wind of change blowing through my hair. . . .

I'll send you a postcard from the good life.

xoxoxo—Goddess

chapter ten

The infamous Tonga Club turned out to be a huge island hot spot with an inconsistent policy regarding ID checks. Hence, the place was packed with perfectly legal twenty-somethings, and then the rest of us, doing our best to look and act older while suppressing our slack-jawed, newbie AWE of the place. Not so successfully, I might add.

In addition to three sweeping bars topped with some expensive wood Lani said was called koa, the place featured a raised, black-lighted dance floor that spilled onto a lanai—basically a huge deck—overlooking a gorgeous swath of beachfront. Multicolored spotlights, perfectly synchronized to the techno beat, cast streams of color across the sand and onto the incoming waves.

Rather than smelling of smoke, sweat, and spilled beer, like most bars, the Tonga Club smelled of fresh ocean air and plumeria blossoms. Okay, *and* spilled beer. But, still. I couldn't help but think one out of three was a vast improvement.

In other words, my first foray into the Hawaiian club scene couldn't have happened in a cooler place. It would probably ruin the simple joy of sneaking into regular old beer joints like the High Noon when I returned to reality, but I'd deal with that when the time came.

Despite the perfect ambiance of Tonga, however, I wasn't having much success cutting loose and enjoying it. The night started out bad, with me stressing about my dad busting us, and it went downhill from there, despite my promise to Jiggy that I'd "just have fun." I don't know . . . maybe my expectations had been too high. I had hoped for a "girls' night out" and wound up "odd girl out" instead.

Lani had abandoned us almost immediately to exchange body shots with a group of guys she seemed to know—some of them VERY well, if you get my gist. When I mentioned that it seemed strange the way Lani had basically disappeared, Jiggy laughed it off, saying that's "just the way it's done."

Really? Because I sort of thought you were supposed to socialize with the friends you came with, silly me. Or, at the very least, meet up between dances to check in, say hey, fan the perspiration off each other's necks, etc.

But, gee, what did I know?

I was the club scene virgin of the group.

In light of this eye-opening bit of knowledge, I suppose

I shouldn't have been surprised when Jiggy basically abandoned ME shortly thereafter to rock the dance floor with one guy after another—in between numerous Jell-O shots, of course. "Abandoned" might be too strong a word, but still. I was bummed, and not *just* about the distinct possibility of Jiggy hurling those Jell-O shots in our stateroom later.

Frankly, I felt like an afterthought, and I vehemently wished I'd just stayed on the ship as per my boring but safe routine. I should say, Jiggy didn't pull a *complete* Lani. She smiled and waved at me from the dance floor often enough, and she *did* try to coax me out there several times. But I didn't want to dance with a bunch of gropey guys, and I figured she ought to know that by now.

Yeah, I was a drag.

I damn well knew it, but I couldn't seem to stop.

I selfishly wished Jiggy would abandon the whole guy hunt for *one* freakin' night and just hang with me. It was our FIRST time in a club underage together, ya know? It should've been a "moment."

No such luck.

So, there I sat, the consummate outsider, slumped behind a tall bar table nursing a watery Diet Pepsi, and clearly sending out sonar-like UNAPPROACHABLE vibes, if my lack of popularity was any indication. Seriously, this was a top-shelf meat market, and yet I hadn't been propositioned by a single guy. Not even a REPULSIVE guy. It had to be some kind of a pathetic record. Not that I *wanted* guys to hit on me, but it was the principle of the matter.

Fickle observation—I know, I KNOW.

Somehow I'd morphed into a gloomy, ugly-ass, old wallflower of the WORST kind, and despite the fact that it made me feel like even more of a monumental buzzkill, I couldn't stop watching Jiggy's spectacle on the dance floor as though I were some freakin' uptight chaperone.

I simply had never witnessed my best friend doing the ol' bump and grind like that before, and I swear she got bumpier and grindier with every shot she threw back. Part of me was impressed with her newfound confidence. She seemed free, wanton, and fun as she laughed and flirted and tossed her blond mane around like some untouchable supermodel. But her out-of-character behavior set off warning alarms in my chest too. The light kept glinting off her exposed belly button jewel, and from the predatory looks all the guys were giving her, I knew they'd taken due notice. They were circling like sharks, and frankly, it freaked my ass out. Jiggy might appear to be worldly and experienced—even to my eyes right then—but she *wasn't*. I mean, talk about a recipe for disaster.

I found the whole situation both eye-opening and surreal, as though I'd somehow missed out on a whole chapter of Jiggy's life lately. Which, considering my bleak mood, launched me into a mental flogging to the tune of "You suck as a friend, Camille," and made me wish the bartender had slipped a shot of rum into my glass along with the lime. I seriously felt like I *had* to go partying with Jiggy from now on. What if something happened to her? Lani might've introduced her little underage protégé to this world, but she was doing a piss-poor job of keeping an eye on her. And, from the looks of Jiggy's behavior, SOMEONE had to.

Grim.

If I had to describe my mood at that moment, "grim" would definitely be my word of choice, with "TRAPPED" coming in as a close second. I checked my watch, wondering how much longer I had to endure this torture before making some excuse, yanking Jiggy to the curb, and grabbing a cab back to the ship.

"Hey!"

I turned toward the voice next to my ear and found Makaio standing there smiling at me. At least, he *was* smiling until he got a load of my evil expression.

"Whoa."

He stepped back, and I took in his super-casual outfit: loose blue board shorts, white tank top, and sandals. He looked freakin' incredible. I was glad I'd gone casual, too, in my denim cutoffs and the Badass Coffee Co. T-shirt I'd picked up in Kona the week before.

"Bad night?" he asked.

"Something like that. Sorry."

"You scared me for a sec." He grinned.

Great. Now I was scary. I glanced down into my glass, circling my index finger in the condensation on the outside. I mean, of *course* he was all easygoing and happy-go-lucky. He lived in PARADISE, and he had a great job where everyone worshipped him. No chance in hell he'd ever wind up on *anyone's* pity-screw list.

Still, he'd done nothing to deserve my wrath.

I twisted my mouth apologetically. "I didn't mean to give you the ol' stink eye."

"No worries. I'm surprised to see you here."

"I'm surprised to be here. Jiggy and Lani dragged me with them."

He glanced around. "Where are they?"

"Dancing, and—" I waved my hand toward Lani, still in the corner with the guys.

"Ah, yes." He shook his head slightly as he watched her. "Look for the biggest, loudest group of guys in any club, and you'll usually find Lani in the middle of them."

I didn't quite know what to make of his comment, and I couldn't read his tone. Amusement? Disgust? A little of both, maybe? In any case, I decided to pump him for info.

He tipped his head toward the unoccupied chair next to me. "Can I?"

I shrugged. "Go for it." Clearly no one *else* wanted to sit there. "So . . . how well do you know Lani?" I asked as he settled in.

"Well enough. Why?"

"What do you think of her?"

He tilted his head side to side. "Smart girl. Very smart. A little wild. *Hemajang*, yah? All mixed up."

No kidding. "Jiggy practically worships her," I said, hoping he'd give me some nugget of insight I could use to pull my pal back from the brink.

"I've noticed," he said, in a tone that effectively ended the questioning. "So. What are you drinking?"

Alrighty, then. No more quizzing. "Rat poison."

His brows rose. "Huh?"

"Oh, my mistake," I quipped, in a snarky tone. "That's just what I *wish* I were drinking."

"Damn, it *is* a bad night." He leaned in, forearms on the table. "Wanna talk about it?"

"Nah. Anyway"—I grimaced, indicating my nearly empty glass—"it's nothing exciting. You don't want to know."

"Sure, I do. That's why I asked."

Big sigh. I was annoyed with myself because I had to fight the urge to explain WHY I wasn't drinking something "cooler" than a soft drink. But I shouldn't have to justify my decision not to booze it up, what with being *seventeen* and all, right? It's not like I was opposed to underage drinking on a global scale, it was just a personal freaking CHOICE on that particular night, and—

Chill, Camille.

I took a deep breath and eased it out slowly. Holy shit, I was arguing with *myself*. Over NOTHING. The guy had asked a simple, harmless question. They had hardcore MEDS for freaks like me. "Diet Pepsi," I muttered finally, quickly adding, "I know. You probably think I'm totally lame," before I could stop myself. My back still prickled with defensiveness.

He pressed his lips together and nodded. "I don't know about lame, but you definitely have questionable taste."

I glanced at him sharply.

He raised his own glass, his dark eyes gleaming playfully.

"I'm firmly in the Coca-Cola camp myself. Never have understood the Pepsi generation, yah?"

Surprised, I smiled—my first genuine smile of the night. "Very funny. News flash: Coke is gross. It tastes like black pepper, and leaves a sweatery coating on your teeth."

"It's the Pepsi poison making you talk all crazy like that," he said, circling a finger around his ear.

"Whatever." My tense shoulders relaxed. I sipped my drink, swallowed, then cleared my throat. Weird how a few moments of light banter could take the edge off, just like that. I suddenly felt as if I had an ally. I scrunched my nose. "So, you're really drinking a Coke?"

"I am."

"Why aren't you having something more exciting?"

"Such as?"

I shrugged. "I don't know. Jell-O shots, piña colada?"

He fake-shuddered. "Girly drinks. Not my thing."

"Okay, then, Jack and Coke," I offered, rolling my eyes. "Or whatever manly men go for. Motor oil. I don't know."

A disconcerting expression moved across Makaio's face, and he ran a hand through his surf-casual hair. "I don't drink much, yah? One now and then, but . . ."

"Why?" I blurted without thinking.

He rolled one muscular shoulder. "I usually volunteer to be the designated driver for the others." He lifted his chin toward a group of people I recognized immediately as crew from the ship.

"Why don't you guys take turns?"

"We just don't," he said in a flat voice.

"Oh." My ego stung, as if I'd crossed some line I hadn't realized existed. "I was just curious. Sorry."

"No, it's all good," he said, before falling quiet for a minute. A muscle in his jaw jumped a few times, as though he were wrestling with something. "Actually . . ."

"Yeah?"

"My older brother was killed in a motorcycle crash." He stared at me dead level. "Drunk. And he killed the driver of the car he hit too."

My stomach contracted with shock. I couldn't even imagine going through something like that, and yet I wouldn't have even suspected Makaio had if he hadn't told me. He always seemed so carefree. "Makaio, I'm . . . I'm so sorry." I touched his arm hesitantly, then felt weird about the contact and pulled back. "I didn't mean to—"

"I know. It's okay."

I flicked my tongue over my suddenly dry lips. "Did it happen recently?"

"Three years ago. But it feels like yesterday."

"Wow." I swallowed thickly.

"Yah." He raised his Coke to me, but the pain still shadowed his eyes. "Not worth it, eh? I'd rather be clear-headed."

I tucked my hair behind my ear, scarcely noticing the hopping club around us anymore. "Do you have . . . um . . . any other brothers or sisters?" I asked, hoping to steer the conversation back to more comfortable ground for him. Or maybe for me—it was hard to tell.

His serious expression eased, and he nodded once. "Two brothers and two sisters. Twin sisters. I'm smack in the middle of the four of them. How about you?"

"Nope. Only child. My parents have such whacked-out jobs, I don't think they could handle the logistics of more than one kid." I sort of laughed. "They could barely handle me, actually."

He sipped his Coke. "What's your mom's deal?"

"She's an archaeologist."

His eyes opened wider. "No lie?"

I shook my head, feeling proud of her. "She's in Argentina, on a dig. That's why I'm here. Well . . . sort of."

"What do you mean?"

I flipped my hand. "The SAT thing."

He leaned his head back, eyes narrowed. "Oh. Right."

"Jiggy and I were supposed to stay in Madison for the summer, but they thought I needed"—I made quotes with my fingers—"parental supervision so I'd study."

"Were they right?"

"Probably," I admitted after a pause, and we both laughed. "Anyway, I'm glad I came. It's cool here."

Makaio adjusted on the stool, leaning back and resting one ankle over the opposite knee. He draped his arm over the back of the empty chair next to him. "How's that going, anyway? The studying."

I swirled my straw absentmindedly in my glass. "Eh,

okay. But I've started dreaming in SAT question format, which is disturbing."

He grinned. "I'm an education major. If you need someone to quiz or coach you, let me know."

My knee-jerk instinct was to refuse, but something made me pause. "Thanks. I will."

"What gave you trouble the first time you took it? If you don't mind me askin'?"

"Oh. Nothing . . . in particular." I stalled. He waited. Dang. "Actually, I sort of got distracted and didn't study. At all."

"That'll do it." He reached over and plicked me on the forehead with his finger and thumb.

"Ow!" I rubbed the spot. "I know, I know. Why do you think I've had my face stuffed in a book all summer?"

"You'll do fine this time around. Jus' don't pressure out, eh?"

I nodded. "That's the plan."

"It's nice to meet someone who actually learned from her mistakes," he said.

GLUG! I pushed away the intrusive thoughts of Brett that plunged straight into my brain like an ice pick.

We sat in comfortable silence for a few moments, and I bounced my feet, concentrated on the bass pounding up from the floor. All of a sudden reality hit me: I couldn't believe I was sitting here with Makaio. More to the point, I couldn't believe I was *glad* to be sitting here with him. It should have sent up all kinds of red flags, but it didn't, which in and of itself was a red flag that I chose to ignore.

"What's that about?" he asked, suddenly, and something in his sharp tone set my heart racing.

I followed his worried gaze to Jiggy, pressed up against some huge, older, rough-looking guy on the dance floor. She seemed a bit stumbly and glazed, and she wasn't smiling anymore. My stress level ratcheted up a notch.

"Shit," I muttered, standing up. "Don't leave," I implored, as I yanked on the hems of my cutoffs. "Okay?"

"Let me." He started to push himself out of his chair, but I laid a hand on his forearm.

"No, it's okay."

"I know that *moke,* Camille. He's bad news."

"I understand, but hang on. She's had too much to drink, is all, and she was probably just flirting."

"So? He's manhandling her."

He strode forward, but I leaped in front of him and pressed both palms against his chest. "Makaio, let me talk to her first. Please?"

I watched him clench his teeth a couple times, most likely considering the wisdom of handling it my way. Finally, he raised both hands in surrender and stepped back. Pushing out a breath, I started toward the dance floor, then stopped. Spun back. Bit my lip. I didn't want to ask, but—

"What now? Go!"

"You won't . . . you won't say anything to my dad, will you?" I felt like the biggest ass EVER in asking him for this particular favor after what he'd confided in me. But I had to. Jiggy was my friend, and I promised I'd always have her back. "I swear, she's not usually like this."

He scowled, as though I'd insulted him with the question—not to mention with the obvious lie. From what he'd seen lately, Jiggy was *exactly* like this. "Just go get her, Camille," he said, in a disgusted tone. "Now. Or I will."

chapter eleven

The worst thing about drunk people, aside from their penchant to puke without warning, is that they just don't know when to SHUT THE HELL UP.

We'd managed to pry Jiggy away from the jerk, although he and Makaio ended up having heated words in the middle of the crowded dance floor after the creep got up in my face a bit. All I remember is him growling at me to "mind my own damn business," lunging so close that I caught his saliva spray. It stunned me immobile and turned my stomach simultaneously.

Before I knew what had hit me, a gentle but firm hand clamped my shoulder, and then I was unceremoniously whipped aside by Makaio. Taking the hint, I grabbed Jiggy and backed off a few feet, grateful for the buffer. I wasn't some cowering wimp, but no way did I want to tangle with some pissed-off, spitting-drunk Samoan guy on my first foray into fake-ID land. Yeah, I'd like to think I'm just a *tad* smarter than that, thank you very much.

Shuddering, I wiped off my face with the crook of my elbow. All around us, the partying continued as though nothing had happened. Dancers jostled into my shoulder and back repeatedly, oblivious. I didn't care, nor did I move out of their way. I was tunnel-visioned on Makaio and the other guy, hoping and praying that Jiggy hadn't stupidly gotten us into an awkward situation that would escalate into something much worse.

I couldn't hear their "conversation" at all over the deafening thump of the music . . . or maybe that was my heartbeat . . . but I swear I didn't blink or take a single breath the whole time they stood rigidly, chest to chest, fists clenched at their sides like weapons to be drawn at a moment's notice. I *so* didn't want them to fight. What if Makaio got in trouble? Or fired? Or hurt? *Oh, God*—what if the other guy had a weapon?

Finally, Makaio must've hit a nerve, because the groper threw up his hands in apparent disgust. He flashed one death glare toward Jiggy—who didn't even notice, she was so out of it—then shouldered his way through the crowd toward one of the bars.

Relief drained through me. I sucked in a breath and clutched the neck of my T-shirt in a shaky hand.

Makaio sought me with his eyes, then jerked his head toward the door. I nodded numbly, hooked my arm with Jiggy's, and stumbled her in that direction, murmuring "uh huh, yeah, uh huh" as she prattled on about God knows what. I couldn't even understand her.

Meanwhile, Makaio wound through the dancers and crossed the club toward Lani. He touched her shoulder, then leaned in and whispered something in her ear. She looked from him to us, then nodded. Just like that. I mean, wouldn't you have thought she'd come running to see whether or not Jiggy was okay? Whatever. I was so *done* with Lani and this whole freakin' train wreck of a night.

After a quick word with Faustino, who appeared to be offering to help, Makaio met us at the entrance.

"Let's get out of here," he said. His pissed-off, urgent tone mirrored the fire in his eyes.

I nodded, my throat still clamped too tightly to speak. We took hold of Jigs and half-carried her as she staggered limply into the packed parking lot. She was in worse shape than I'd realized.

"Why didn't you tell me things had gotten this out of control?" Makaio growled. His heated glare over Jiggy's bowed head stung like a slap.

The subtle accusation rang in my ears, and guilt nearly suffocated me. I forced a swallow past the lump of pain that had lodged in my esophagus. "I . . . I didn't know." A pathetic answer, for sure. Jiggy was supposedly my best friend. So, how come I'd been too self-absorbed to notice her dangerous downward-spiral? I saw it happening, and yet I didn't. I discounted, rationalized, accepted, made excuses. But I hadn't stepped in to find out what was really going on. So much about that just wasn't right.

Makaio didn't berate me, like he no doubt wanted to. Instead, he shook his head once, jaw clenched.

"I'm sorry." My voice caught on the apology. "I should've taken better notice."

"No. Not your fault."

Yeah, and that's exactly what it felt like when he'd snapped at me a minute ago. NOT.

"Damn Lani," he muttered to himself.

That surprised me. "Did she ever mention anything about—?" I lifted my chin toward Jiggy.

He shook his head. "If she had, none of this would've happened, believe me."

Jiggy drooped, seeming to almost pass out, but we caught her weight. My stomach swirled. "Is she going to be okay?"

"I hope so. We'll find out as soon as Doc looks at her."

The ship's doctor meant my dad would know too. But I couldn't even argue with the decision. Jiggy was *that* drunk.

Repeating instructions and encouragement as though speaking to a child, we struggled to pour a mostly incoherent Jiggy into the back of the weathered old Ford Fiesta Makaio had borrowed to chauffeur everyone that evening. Which reminded me— "How's everyone getting back to the ship?"

"Don't worry about that right now, yah? Just take care of your friend."

I nodded. Behind us, the surf crashed in and out, reliable as always. The muffled beat of the music reached out like crooked fingers each time the club's door opened. Once we had her safely inside the car, floppy limbs and all, I grabbed the seat belt.

"You got that?"

"Yeah." I flicked a quick glance at him over my shoulder. I wrangled Jiggy into the stupid restraint—no easy feat since she'd slumped over on her side in a loose, awkward pile. God, how many shots had she done, anyway? Hadn't she ever heard the phrase "know your limit"?

Makaio circled the car and got in, kicking the engine to life. He pressed a button, and all the windows lowered to allow in the cool tropical air.

I tugged on Jiggy's seat belt to make sure it had latched beneath her, then paused, suddenly struck by the awful picture before me.

A swirl of protectiveness flipped my tummy. I reached into the car and brushed Jiggy's hair out of her face, gently. With the pad of my thumb, I wiped a smudge of mascara from beneath her eye. She looked like shit, and it actually hurt seeing her like this—dead center in my chest, like someone had stomped there, leaving the imprint of a Doc Marten boot sole on my flesh. My bottom lip started quivering, so I clamped it between my teeth. Hard. This wasn't the time to lose control.

But I felt . . . God . . . so horrible.

I'd carried on as if I were the only person suffering this summer, but clearly that wasn't true. I'd just . . . missed it somehow. But how was I supposed to know? Jiggy had seemed *happier* since we got here, not sadder. I mean, she was having a blast, crushing on a million guys—

And then the obvious hit me.

Happier, my ass. She'd been practically manic. I clenched my fists, silently castigating myself for having failed her so profoundly.

DUH, had I ever stopped to think that, perhaps, her über-happiness might just be a cover for how she was really feeling? Kind of like my tendency to employ a touch of sarcasm now and then to hide my own annoying vulnerabilities? I know I'd *told* her to forget all the issues with her parents for the summer, but was it really that easy? Had it been that easy for *me* to forget Brett?

What an idiot I'd been.

"Let's hit it," Makaio said.

"Yeah. Okay." I still teetered on the verge of losing it, but things could go either way. I just needed to tough it out until we got back to the ship.

With a deep, fortifying breath, I locked her in, then slid into the front passenger seat. The slamming of my door was like an exclamation point on the end of a long horror-flick scream. Carefully monitoring my emotions, I eased out an exhale.

Makaio threw the transmission into reverse and backed out, the gravel crunching beneath the tires.

Overwhelmed, I dropped my face into my hands and closed my eyes against the sudden and unwelcome sting of tears. The soft breeze ruffled the sleeve of my T-shirt.

Breathe, I commanded. *In . . . out. In . . . out.*

I didn't want Makaio to see how shaken I was.

"Holy shit," I said, the words breathy and muffled by my palms. I felt his hand, warm against my back, and the tenderness of the contact was almost too much to bear.

"You okay?"

"No."

"Camille?" Worry laced his tone.

"I don't know. I'm fine." I groaned, girding my resolve. I refused to break down, at least until I could do so in privacy. "What a nightmare. I knew she'd been partying a lot, but . . ."

"It's over, yah?"

"I wish." I reflected on Jiggy's ridiculous virginity plan. Part of me wondered what would happen next, but the other part was afraid to find out. "You don't know the half of it."

He remained silent for several long moments as we waited for a light to turn green. When it did, he started forward and said, "Well, it's over for tonight, at least."

I wanted to be grateful for small favors. I really did. And speaking of small favors—"I'm glad you didn't fight that guy."

He frowned. "I never intended to fight him."

"Could've fooled me. All the yelling at each other, and the fists. Your freakin' knuckles were white." I raked both hands through my hair, wiggling my fingers through the wind-tangled curls. "You scared the crap out of me."

"Look, I only would've fought him if I'd had to. That's not really my thing."

He waited for me to speak, probably to say I knew he wasn't the bar brawl type, whatever.

When I didn't say anything, his tone sharpened. "You'd rather I sat there and watched while he shoved you around?"

"No. Of course not. That's not it." I met his gaze in the dark car. "Thank you. Really. I just don't want to be responsible for . . . causing you problems."

He shrugged off my gratitude, refocusing on the winding road ahead. "You know, you don't control everything in the world, Camille. If I'd chosen to . . . take different steps, I would've caused my own problems. Okay?"

"Okay. Fine." Whatever. Shoot me for trying to be nice.

"Cam?" Jiggy slurred from behind me.

I shifted in my seat to halfway face her, clutching the shoulder strap of my seat belt in my fist. The passing streetlights strobed over her pale face and glistened against the sheen of sweat on her upper lip. "Do you need us to stop? Are you going to puke?"

"No, no. No puking." She waved her hand at me before letting it drop to the seat in front of her face. After a moment, she rubbed it clumsily against her mouth. "It was gonna be okay, Cam. I was fine. He mighta been the guy."

Jesus, not *that*. Disbelief warred with annoyance inside me. You'd think tonight's events would be enough of a wake-up call for her, but apparently not. "He wasn't," I said, toneless, turning away from her.

"What's she talking about?"

"Nothing." I stared straight ahead, unseeing.

"No . . . really," Jiggy said. "You'da liked him. I swear, he wasn't an'thing like Brett."

Every bit of breath left my body in a rush, as if she'd kicked me in the stomach. Reaching out blindly, I gripped the door handle and struggled to maintain my composure. Oh, my GOD, I couldn't BELIEVE she'd actually gone there. Adrenaline shot through my veins, and my gaze jerked to Makaio's face as he stopped at a corner. He didn't seem to be paying much attention, but after all these weeks working together, I knew him better than that. He was the type who sat back and took it *all* in, always.

I cleared my throat, but my voice still wavered when I said, "Don't worry about it, Jigs. Just relax, okay? Don't talk." *Please, God, don't talk.*

"Are y' mad?"

"No," I said, a bit too loudly. My harsh tone belied my words, and panic bubbled inside me. "Just go to sleep."

For a few moments, we sat in blessed silence. I prayed harder than I ever had before that she would simply pass out and let it drop. I'd finally gotten to a place with Makaio where I didn't feel like an idiot every single second I was around him. That was huge for me. I desperately did not want him to know about the Brett situation. EVER. Heat spread over my skin just imagining the humiliation that would cause. He would never look at me in the same way. I mean, *I* didn't even look at *myself* in the same way.

"Didya have fun?" Jiggy asked suddenly.

My head throbbed. I bowed it forward and pressed

fingers to the bridge of my nose. "No. I didn't."

"Oh, Cam, you hafta let the Brett thing go. It's been months," she slurred, completely oblivious to the REAL reason my night had sucked.

My whole body tensed. "Jiggy. SHUT. UP."

"What?" she wailed.

"Stop talking." I crossed my arms tightly over my chest. This wasn't happening. It could NOT be happening. I reached up to push the blowing hair back from my forehead, my motions jerky and fierce.

"Who's Brett?" Makaio asked, his confusion clear.

"No one," I said in a low voice, hoping Jiggy couldn't hear us. "Don't listen to her. She has no idea what she's talking about. She's shitfaced."

"But, she said—"

"Who cares what she said? She's rambling, Makaio. For God's sake, let it go."

Jiggy stirred again in the backseat. She tried to sit up, then slumped back down on one elbow. I squeezed my eyes shut. *Don't talk. Don't talk. Don't talk.*

"He's such an ass, M'kaio. Did Cam ev'r tell you 'bout what Brett did to her?"

"No," he said, just as I whipped around and yelled, "Goddamnit, Jiggy! Lie down and shut the fuck up. I am not kidding!" I swear, at that moment, I wanted to reach back between the bucket seats and just choke her.

"You d'serve better than—"

"Jesus!" I leaned forward and smacked the radio on, cranking the volume up so loud, it actually hurt to listen to it. Heavy metal pounded through the vehicle, vibrating every surface. I felt Makaio looking at me, but ignored him. My chest rose and fell rapidly. I needed to scream. I had the crazy urge to jump out of the car and start running. Hard and fast, until my throat burned and my lungs ached. Until I collapsed in the sand on the other side of the island, or the other side of the world. Until I'd outrun this whole fiasco of a summer.

After one song, Makaio slowly reached forward and lowered the volume. "You mind?"

I flashed him a quick sidelong glance. "No."

Behind us, Jiggy'd fallen into a sloppy snore. Too little, too freakin' late.

Makaio touched my leg. "Camille."

"What?" I snapped. I just couldn't handle sympathy right now. Or questions. Or much of anything.

"Look at me."

I hiked my chin and blew him off.

"Please?"

After a huff of frustration, I glared in his direction.

"What is up with you?" he asked softly.

I merely shook my head—one angry jerk side to side—then stared out the window at the dark ocean curving alongside us. Salty warm air whipped against my cheeks, and I welcomed the sting.

All these weeks of fighting to feel stronger, to overcome what had happened in Madison, and it came down to one too many Jell-O shots for my cover to be blown? The whole night was such bullshit. Unbidden, the tears returned, spilling over before I could get a handle on them. I smeared the back of one hand against my cheek furiously.

He cleared his throat. "Whatever it is," he said gently, "it's okay."

I barked out a humorless, watery laugh. "Like you know."

"I do. I know you. And you're okay."

Whatever. He knew the me I'd chosen to put forth.

"You *are*, Cam. That's all that matters."

I lifted my hand, fending off further impromptu therapy. "Please. Just . . . drop it, okay?"

Long pause.

"Okay. If you're sure you don't want to talk about it. I'm a good listener."

If he only knew HOW sure I was. I leaned back against the headrest and closed my eyes. "She's finally out, thank God," I murmured. "Let's just be grateful for the silence." But all the unanswered questions hung between us. Could the current silence ever make up for all Jiggy had revealed?

www.NobodyGetsJiggy.com

Sorry for the blog delay. I haven't been at work for two days now, hence, no computer access. Remember I said I thought something big might happen at the club the other night? Yeah, well, I underestimated myself. Several MAJOR things happened. Namely:

1. *Alcohol poisoning*. Or at least, close to it. I'm not going to reveal what my blood alcohol level was when M dragged me off to the ship's doctor to be tested, but let me just say (a) I deserved to be fronted like that; and (b) the recovery has NOT been fun. AT F-ING ALL. If I never have another Jell-O shot, it will be too soon. I can't even think about Jell-O now without wanting to hurl.

2. *Disappointing C's Dad*. You're thinking, big deal, right? Well, I don't feel that way. C's dad has always considered me "good for" his daughter—a positive influence. Who am I kidding—he's always treated me like a second daughter, and sometimes when my own parents bummed me out, his welcoming inclusion felt really, REALLY good. God. Just seeing the disappointment in his eyes when he came to check on me The Morning After was a crushing blow. He totally trusted me. I guess I hadn't realized how much I'd been taking advantage of that trust, but now I've ruined everything. Initially, he held C accountable, too, until I went and talked to him alone and explained the real deal. C had NOTHING to do with my behavior. And she didn't drink at all, specifically because she didn't want to break her dad's rules. If she and M hadn't been there . . . shit. I can't even contemplate what could've happened. <shudder> Anyway, I laid it all out to him—good, bad, and ugly—so he'd truly understand how desperately I wanted to

avoid dragging C down with me. I'm sure he's going to tell my parents, and you know what? I deserve that.

3. *Launching my career as a public spectacle.* Not only did I, apparently, carry on like a giant TRAMP in the club, but I almost hooked up with a THIRTY-YEAR-OLD creep who has a beer gut and a criminal record. Did I know any of this when we were dancing? No. Does it matter? Uh, no. I still came off like a purely immature idiot in the eyes of all my coworkers, not to mention what C and M think of me. As for L, well, I'm thinking I can't hack it in her big league anymore.

4. *Putting several people in danger as they tried to save my stupid ass.* I'm the most ashamed about M, especially after what C told me happened to his brother. I mean, how can I EVER justify my behavior to him? Let's face it: I can't. UGH. Worst of all . . .

5. *Friendship Destruction.* I am ashamed to admit I committed the MOST egregious of confidentiality breaches while in my drunken stupor, and the worst part is, I don't even remember doing it. C is still furious with me, and I can't blame her one little bit. She claims to have forgiven me, since I was basically blacked out when it all went down, and that's cool, but the forgetting is going to take much longer.

To make matters worse, we found out the next

morning that Grandma T's itinerary had changed, and we weren't going to be able to see her this summer after all. C talked to her on the phone, but it wasn't the same. That was what finally pushed C over the edge completely. I'm not kidding, she sobbed on her bed in our stateroom for HOURS, and she wouldn't even let me console her.

I'm just so scared that things between us will never be the same. . . .

FROM: HurricaneCamille@midwestacademy.wi.edu
TO: YearlingPhD@gorillas-inc.org
TIME: 6:54:11 p.m., HST
SUBJECT: Just so you know

Hi, Louis—

It's Camille, Jiggy's best friend. You don't know this, but your little sister has been writing you long, heartfelt e-mails and then deleting them for a LONG time. I've told her for YEARS to just suck it up and talk to you about her turmoil, but she won't. She bottles up her feelings—maybe you know that about her? Anyway, some stuff has happened this summer, and I really think she needs her brother. I'm not trying to be disloyal or vengeful by coming to you behind her back, and I'm not sending you these links so you can judge her or bust her. So I hope you won't. I just think you deserve to know how much she's struggling.

www.NobodyGetsJiggy.com
www.TheTruthAboutBrett.com

Fair warning: She's going to be flaming pissed when she finds out I sent this e-mail. But friends don't let friends go off the deep end without at least ONE cry for help, so I'm ready to face that. I hope all is well in Rwanda. Kiss a gorilla for me. (If you're allowed to, that is.)

Sincerely,

Camille Tafoya

chapter twelve

According to the law of physics, for every action there is an equal and opposite reaction. That sort of describes what happened to our lives in the few weeks after Tonga Club Hell Night. It went something like this:

ACTION: Jiggy ran her freakin' mouth in the car, as we all know, effectively fronting me off to the ONE person who I'd hoped would never know ANYTHING about what that dickhead, Brett, had perpetrated back home.

REACTION: I've never been so furious in my life. At least since the whole Brett thing went down. So . . .

ACTION: I took it upon myself to send Jiggy's brother, Louis, links to her blogs. Frankly, someone needed to snap a knot in her ass, and I was running out of resources. Plus, I really was worried about her after everything that had happened. Not to mention, she deserved it.

REACTION: Louis was beyond alarmed. So,

ACTION: He contacted Jiggy, seemingly out of the blue, which thrilled her. Until he raised his concerns about her lifestyle, of late.

REACTION: Jiggy became totally defensive and suspicious, firing questions at him like a seasoned interrogator. So . . .

ACTION: Louis, ever the smooth and sophisticated older man (NOT), rolled on me. Well, he didn't mean to. He just OVEREXPLAINED everything, unwittingly busting our cover. I mean, Jigs is no dummy. Initially he told her he'd stumbled upon her blog, read it, and had grown concerned. It might've worked, but then he brought up the OTHER blog. When she realized he'd not only visited NobodyGetsJiggy.com, but TheTruthAboutBrett.com, too, she puzzled it out. Only two people knew for sure that she was connected to the anonymous Brett blog: (1) me; and (2) Lani. Since Lani has been on her BEST behavior ever since the formal reprimand she received from my father, Jiggy knew I'd outed her.

REACTION: She confronted me. And—

ACTION: I admitted it. Frankly, I felt relieved to admit it. It would've sucked having that secret between us forever, you know?

REACTION: Jiggy was initially SO PISSED that I'd contacted Louis behind her back, she couldn't even see straight. She also couldn't see that I'd done it to *help* her, not hurt her. She confronted me on the deck surrounding the Teens Only pool, and our "words" had quickly escalated to a shoving match. We'd graduated to round one of a full-blown fistfight before long—ME AND JIGGY! The teen cruise directors had to pull us off each other and shove us into the pool to break it up. It was so insane. So, since Jiggy didn't get the pleasure of fully pounding my face in as she'd wanted to . . .

ACTION: She marched right over and gave Makaio the skinny on what had actually happened between Brett and me.

Oh, yeah. SO not kidding. And SO utterly wrong.

To make matters even MORE intolerable, I learned of this felonious breach of the Universal Friendship Pact from the worst possible person, Makaio, and while in the worst possible position of vulnerability.

I'd stopped by the fitness deck that afternoon because (1) I was done studying for the day; (2) Jigs and I weren't exactly on SPEAKING terms after the WWF gig at the pool, so I couldn't chill in the room; and (3) I had yet to master the advanced climbing route that included that dang roof. I didn't want to leave the ship without doing so.

Faustino was just packing up his stuff for the day, having a few final words with Makaio when I approached. We were on the tail end of a Silver Fox theme cruise, so all the cruisers were age seventy-five and older. Hence, the climbing wall had been incredibly slow all week, while shuffleboard and bingo were standing-room-only each and every day. Perfect time to tackle that route. "Hey," I said to my coworkers.

"What's up?" Makaio asked, smiling. Both he and

Faustino seemed happy to see me there. We'd grown into a comfortable, easy camaraderie over the summer. I'd never admit it out loud, but I'd really grown to like the guy. If I was in the market for LIKE, he'd totally be number one on my shopping list. I felt a sense of pride for resisting the urge to hit on him.

"Nothing." I squinted up at the wall, hands on my hips. "Just thought I'd give that climb another try."

"Cool. I'll belay."

"I am going, unless you guys need me to stay," Faustino said. He hiked his cruise line logo duffel on his shoulder and raised a hand for a quick salute.

"Naw, brah. It's all good." Makaio gave him a jovial clap on the back. "I'll see you there later tonight, yah?"

"Wouldn't miss it." Faustino winked at me. "You can get this climb, Camille. Just don't psych yourself out."

"Thanks. Bye." I waggled my fingers as he left. When it was just Makaio and me, I wound my hair into a knot at the nape of my neck and asked, "What's going on later tonight? Not that it's any of my business." I stepped into a bright yellow safety harness and began to click in and check the knots.

"Poker night," he said with a grin, preparing and checking the belay system. "Guys only."

"Why? You have strippers there or something?"

He shook his head. "I'm sorry to burst your bubble, Camille, but not all of us guys are that way."

"Whatever." I softened the word with a playful smile, but I *did* wonder what would've made him say THAT. I wasn't always spouting anti-guy sentiment, at least not in front of him. To reiterate: whatever.

I hooked in and walked to the wall, glancing up while trying to recall my route choices from my last failed attempt. I didn't want to do the same thing over and over, expecting a different result. Wasn't that the definition of insanity?

I stepped in and curled my hand around the first bucket, then peered over my shoulder. "You ready for me?"

"Yep. Belay on."

"Climbing."

"Ho'o mau!"

After that, I concentrated on making the best choices for my route, occasionally working my way into a dead end and having to back off and try again. Makaio provided constant encouragement, and the occasional suggestion to "grab the chickenhead to your left" or "stem with your right foot before you go for that one."

The first part of the climb was fairly easy, but then I got near that damn roof and my skills seemed to shrink. There weren't as many holds up here, so the choices I made had more immediate consequences. It's where I always got tripped up. I tried to breathe through it.

"You're clean so far, Cam."

I nodded. My forearms were fried, though. "Got me? I need to rest for a sec."

"Yep." Immediately I felt the slack leave the rope.

I sat back, then flexed and relaxed my arms while

staring up at the roof. I just needed to make the right decisions here—grab for the correct holds, not just the closest or most obvious.

I mean, how hard could it be?

"So . . . Jiggy's here," Makaio said in a tentative voice.

"Huh," I said, using my So Not Interested tone, even though I sort of was. But, why should I care? Makaio knew all about what had transpired at the pool. Shoot, practically the whole SHIP knew what had gone down, at least crew-wise. Plus, he'd been there to witness the ugliest of all ugly nights. He knew more than anyone how unexpectedly rocky things had become between Jiggy and me. So why the sudden need to inform me of her whereabouts?

Guys. I swear.

Still, curiosity took hold. "So . . . here where?"

"On the track."

Against my will, I craned my neck around. Sure enough. Jiggy wore her pink iPod on her right upper arm as she walked swiftly up the starboard side of the track. Weird. I was still pissed, but she looked just like my bestest friend in the whole universe, and something inside my chest warmed. Part of me wanted to run over there, just to say hey. Like nothing had happened. Like life was All Good. You know, make the first step to get past this crap we'd fallen into and move forward.

Another part of me wanted to turn back to my climb and forget Makaio had ever said a word about her. I paused, cleared my throat. "Why's she here?"

"Uh, for fitness?" he said in a Big Duh voice.

I cast him a droll stare. We both knew Jiggy hadn't spent much time on the fitness deck so far this summer. She just wasn't as into it as I was, which was fine. Everyone had their own thing.

"Actually, she came to talk to me, yah?"

Huh. Interesting. Annoyingly so. But, frankly, I wanted to climb, not launch into an impromptu friendship-counseling session or whatever weirdness was going on here. "That's great. You got me?"

He stared at me for several long moments, then sighed. "Belay on."

"Climbing."

"Climb on."

Pushing the Jiggy talk out of my head, I re-engaged with my game plan. I jammed my right foot in a crevice, then grabbed for a bucket that was almost too far away. On my second try, I got it. With a breath of relief, I moved on, ever closer to my goal of conquering this route. But I couldn't give it my full concentration. Curiosity pecked at me again, like an overeager bird. Or, a whole flock of them. I braced my foot on a hold and pushed up. "So, um . . . what did she want to talk about? Let me guess . . . about how much I suck as a friend?"

"No." He paused, and then, just as I'd pulled a dyno for a hold I had yet to ever reach, he added, "She told me about what happened with that dude. Brett."

I actually yelled. Or yelped. Damn good thing I was wearing safety restraints, because my limbs went weak and I almost lost my grip. I missed the hold and pulled a gigantic barn door off the side of the wall. That is, until my other foot slipped and I fell off altogether. Makaio caught the slack and held me.

I bounced there, stupified for a moment, while my blood literally ran cold, and then just as quickly ripped into a full, rolling boil. My fingers tingled, and it had nothing at all to do with the exertion. I glared down as my humiliation ballooned up, bigger and bigger, until it exploded into sheer, blinding rage. "Get me off of this wall. Now."

Makaio hesitated, pleading with his eyes. "Camille, just talk to me for a minute. It's okay—"

"Screw you!" I yelled, anger bringing hot tears to blur my vision. I flailed about for something to throw, but of course there was nothing. My hair came loose from its knot and whipped into my face with the breeze. "Don't tell me what to do!"

"I'm not. I'm just . . . Cam, I'm not letting you down until you relax. And talk to me. Please."

"No! This is my life! It has nothing to do with you *or* Jiggy. I am not talking to you about this, and you're not going to dangle me up here like your damn prisoner—"

"Cam, please!"

"NOW!" I spoke through clenched teeth. "Let me down now, damn it, or I swear to God I'm going to unhook." I laid my hand on the biner. "I'm not kidding, Makaio."

He held up one hand in surrender. "Okay. Okay. Just hang on. Stop talking crazy," he said, blowing out a frustrated breath as he lowered me with some urgency. Every few feet or so, he'd stop and say, "Camille, please," or, "She wasn't trying to hurt you," only continuing to lower me when I threatened again to unhook.

LIES, all of it.

Of all people, Jiggy knew how important it was to me that Makaio never learn what an IDIOT I'd been back home. Whatever comfort level I'd established with Makaio was now gone—POOF—just like that, thanks to Jiggy and her big mouth. The whole situation was as unbelievable as it was unforgivable.

The minute my feet touched the ground, I unhooked and took off in a sprint toward the running track, the harnass I still wore clacking and jerking, making it awkward to run. I could hear Makaio calling for me, but I ignored him. Jiggy and I were going to have it out, once and for all.

Right here.

Right now.

I'd been as good a friend to her as I possibly could be, and this was how she paid me back?

Jiggy went down hard when I tackled her from behind, the breath pushing from her lungs in a surprised OOF. I felt her muscles tense from the unexpected attack, but I hung tough as she struggled. She flailed against me. I rolled her over and yanked the iPod headphones from her ears. A scrape on her chin from the rough texture of the track started to bleed.

I forced myself to ignore it. "You bitch! How could you, Jiggy? How?!"

Regaining her strength, she bucked me off her and crab-scrambled backward a few feet, then stopped, swiping at her chin, then studying her hand. Her gaze flashed up at me, incredulous and pissed. "Jesus, I'm bleeding! What the hell is the matter with you?" She lunged forward and shoved my chest.

I shoved back—HARD—then pounced on top of her, holding her shoulders down with the heels of my hands. "I thought you were my friend!"

"I *am* your friend, idiot!" She wrenched one shoulder out from under my hand and used my momentary unsteadiness to land a ringing slap on my cheek.

Stunned, I sat back and reached up to hold my face.

"I suppose you don't remember that you fronted me off to my brother," she said, bucking me twice before rolling to the side and dumping me off. She rushed to stand. "And that wasn't a betrayal?"

My cheek still burned, but I jumped up, too, and surged forward to relaunch the ass-kicking. "I told him because I was worried about you, and you're too damn annoying to do it yourself. I did you a favor!"

"God, Camille!" She grabbed the harness and twisted me down to my knees, then toppled me. "Everything is so one-sided with you."

"That's crap!" I reached up to slap her, but she grabbed my wrist. We muscled against each other to no avail. "Talking to Louis doesn't compare in ANY way to you telling Makaio. Louis is your *brother*."

"So what?"

We rolled to the side, over and over, grunting and swearing. "So, he cares about you!"

"News flash, dumbass: Makaio cares about you, too."

"God!" I balled my fist and pulled back, preparing to nail her right in the face, but my elbow was gripped from behind. Before I could react, Makaio wrapped his hand around the back of my harness and yanked me easily off Jiggy. Not before she laid a sucker punch right on my cheekbone, however.

He set me on my feet but held me back. "It's true, Cam," Makaio said, his eyes flashing. "I do care. And I couldn't care *less* about some asshole guy back home, okay?" He jerked his chin at Jiggy. "Get up."

She did.

"Cut this shit out. Both of you." He looked from me to Jiggy, then back to me. "I'm not kidding. Be pissed off, if you want to, but stop acting like kids. You're *both* guilty, and you're *both* wrong. You're also both *right*."

I eased off, and he let me go.

"I'm sorry," Jiggy told Makaio. "I didn't mean for this to happen."

He shook his head to the side once, then looked at me. "Take the harness off," he said, in a gentler voice. "You two need to go to your separate corners and cool off. Don't make me go to the captain."

Dang. Low blow. I could feel my eye swelling as I undid the harness with shaky hands and passed it over to him.

"I'm not as stupid as the whole Brett thing makes me sound," I muttered.

"The only person who ever blamed you for that is *you*."

I peered up at him.

"Jiggy didn't." He gestured toward her.

I blinked over and saw that she'd begun to cry, silently. Her chin still bled. My stomach clenched.

"I didn't either. And I'm *glad* she told me. It explained a lot."

"What's that supposed to mean?"

Makaio shook his head sadly. "Figure it out." And then he turned and walked away.

Jiggy and I stared at each other for a moment or two before we spun away and left the fitness deck too. I felt bad about the cut on her chin. But then I reached up and felt the gigantic lump that used to be my eye socket. Damn. I was going to have a shiner.

And Makaio knew about Brett.

And my best friend probably hated my guts.

Life sucked.

chapter thirteen

So, the shiner was huge.

But my homicidal urge dissipated pretty quickly when I came to the stunning realization that Makaio was actually IMPRESSED with how I'd handled the Brett aftermath. <insert utter shock here> It didn't seem to color his feelings about me, except in a good way. He told me the day after the fight that, in his mind, Brett was a worthless excuse for a person and a disgrace to all guys, which of course I already knew. He also told me I was strong, resilient, brave, smart, etc.—you know, all those attributes I used to associate with Lani (USED TO being the operative phrase).

I felt so utterly unburdened now that (1) my ugly secret had been exposed; and (2) it hadn't destroyed my life like I'd expected, that I actually decided to give in and agree to go climb that damned waterfall with Makaio and his friends.

He completely surprised me by refusing to take me unless I brought Jiggy along. After ALL these weeks of accusing me of being too afraid to try it. CAN YOU BELIEVE THE FREAKIN' GALL? I sputtered and argued, listing all the wrongs Jiggy had perpetrated against me in recent days, pointing out my gigantic black eye. Know what he said? "*E nā nā `oe i kou iho*, Camille," to which I replied, "Oh, great. Throw Hawaiian at me in my moments of great stress, why don't you?" to which HE replied (with a smile), "It means, 'Look at yourself first.'"

Uncool.

Okay, sure. He'd nailed it. Neither of us was innocent. I'd committed a few acts of evil against Jigs, too. Still. Makaio was so determined to mediate Jigs and me through this rocky stretch in our friendship. Forced proximity was his weapon of choice. I admit it: I gave in. Frankly, I was feeling so globally benevolent at that point, what with the burden of my Brett secret lifted, I felt an urgency, as well as a strong desire, to patch things up too. In light of all that had happened, I knew Jiggy and I needed to talk things out. Preferably before we returned to Madison, which would happen in less than three weeks, believe it or not. So I agreed. Let's face it: Our recent bitchfest aside, I'd never had a closer or more important friend than Jiggy, and I loved her. She understood me better than I understood myself most of the time. I wanted to do that for her, too. Plus, if I was going to head off to some romantic waterfall with a bunch of guys, I both needed and wanted her with me as a counterbalance.

So that's how we ended up seated side-by-side on a blanket at the base of the waterfall, in the lushest and most breathtaking valley I had ever seen in my life.

But, let me back up. We started the morning, actually, at the upper ridge overlooking the valley. Makaio, Faustino, and the others insisted the extra several-mile hike was required, extolling the virtues of viewing the valley from the top before attempting the climb. Jiggy and I were dubious, but what the hell? Who knew if we'd ever return there.

We'd parked our three-car caravan along an unassuming and unmarked dirt road, then the whole line of us climbed over or under fences to traverse the private farmland that led to the trailhead. It all appeared so ordinary, at that point. Even the subsequent hike through the dense rain forest, cool as it was, gave no clue to what lay ahead. Seriously, one minute we were on a muddy trail in the woods, and the next *instant* we emerged at the upper edge of a sheer drop into the deep, deep valley. If you weren't paying attention, you could easily take one step too many and plunge to your death.

All of us stood there in total awe, even Makaio and the others who'd been born and raised in the area. Thanks to the recent rain, there wasn't just one waterfall, but several, each one streaming to the base of a gorge so bottomless, you couldn't even hear the splash. WOW.

I mean, I wouldn't have believed someplace so enchanting actually existed outside the pages of a fairy tale. To me, it felt like a magical rain forest. I half-expected little groups of surf-gnomes and hula-fairies to suddenly appear before us.

We snapped a few pictures, oohed and ahhed, then hiked back out the way we'd come. Piling into the cars, we headed quickly to the base of the waterfall. The perspective from the bottom was completely different, but just as impressive and magical. Huge Hawaiian ginger plants surrounded us, with their distinctive plumes of yellow and red flowers that reminded me of July Fourth fireworks.

Jiggy had taken one look at the sheer rock wall behind the super-high waterfall and politely bowed out of the climb. My heart had clutched too, when I saw it, but I'd decided to reserve judgment until I watched some of the guys go for it.

Free-soloing here could be suicide, but Makaio swore that the aid climb to the waterfall jump-off point was totally safe. His climbing club had placed the fixed pro—protection, that is—themselves.

"Bombers," he'd said proudly. "Every one of them."

They'd been totally precise in their placement because, apparently, you had to unhook and jump from a specific, well-marked point in order to hit the water at the right spot and avoid cratering to an ugly, newsworthy death. It definitely looked like a pumpy climb, but . . . I'd just never done anything like it. I couldn't quite make myself commit.

It was Faustino who changed my mind.

I must say, the dude might fall more toward the geeky

end of the guy spectrum, but he was a freakin' superhero when it came to climbing. He must've been born without the fear gene. In any case, he cheerily offered to head up first to check for any manky bolts or other problems—in other words, he volunteered to be the guinea pig. Totally surefooted, he stuck to that face like a tree frog. He totally rallied the climb, reaching the jump point quickly and with zero problems. He made it look easy. Jiggy and I didn't take our eyes off him the whole way.

"Oh, my God," Jiggy whispered as he maneuvered his body to face the water. "How can he just hang there and do that?"

"No kidding."

Just then, Faustino released a war cry that echoed through the valley, unclipped, and dropped like a lawn dart. The moment he started to fall, Jiggy sucked in a breath and covered her face with both hands. She didn't look again until she heard his stoked cheer several seconds after the giant splash he made when his body hit the water.

Emerging exhilarated, Faustino whipped his hair around in that total GUY way and called, "Camille, you have to do it."

I paused for the briefest of seconds. "Okay."

"Serious?" Makaio asked, looking down at me from where he stood, a few feet to my left.

I nodded, indicating Jiggy with a slight tilt of my head. "But you go on. Let me watch a few more people first."

What I really meant was, my best friend and I need time alone to clear the air.

Makaio nodded, then all the guys headed off toward the water's edge. We followed their progress for a minute, then Jiggy pulled her knees up to her chest. She wrapped her arms around her legs and rested her cheek on her knee, facing me.

Moment of truth.

My heart started to pound.

"I'm sorry about your black eye."

I reached out to touch it gingerly. "It's a gooder, that's for sure. I'm sorry about your chin."

"It's okay. Maybe I deserved it." A long pause ensued. "I'm really sorry things didn't work out with Grandma T," she said, quirking her mouth to the side.

"Yeah, that sucked." I scratched my chin. Knots of tension that had been caught up in my muscles since that night at the club started loosening. It was just me and Jigs, like regular old times. What had I been so afraid of? Taking a tentative step forward, I said, "I guess she and the new hubby might move here."

She arched her brows. "For good?"

I nodded. "They love it."

"I can understand that." Another uncomfortable pause stretched between us. "Plus, that would give you the perfect reason to come back. Besides Makaio, I mean."

I swallowed. "The perfect reason for *us* to come back," I told her softly.

Jiggy sighed, squeezing her eyes shut for a second.

Then she started to cry. "I'm so sorry, Cam. For everything. I never meant for things to get so out of hand."

"Would you really have slept with that guy?"

She wiped the heels of her hands underneath her eyes. "Probably, I'm ashamed to say. If you guys hadn't been there to save me. I mean, Lani encouraged me."

Lani. I shook my head. I'd actually begun to feel sorry for her. "But, why?"

She sniffed loudly. "I don't know. Everything started to scare me. That it's our last year of school. The way I felt about my parents. What had happened to you . . . and to Lani." A pause. "Don't blame her too much, Camille. She has her problems too."

"I know." I picked at a loose thread on the blanket. "You know, your parents love you."

"I know. I'm trying to know." She hiked one shoulder.

"They do."

She didn't argue. "I've made a mess of things."

"So what? Shit happens. We just have to learn from our mistakes. Misstep, correction. Over and over." My dad would've been so smug right then, had he heard me.

"Yeah. Have you learned from yours?"

"I hope so. I'm sure trying to. But it doesn't mean I won't make new mistakes."

For a moment, we watched the climber making his way up to the jump point. Jiggy turned to me. "I don't regret telling Makaio what happened to you. Sorry."

"It's okay. I don't regret it either. Now, at least."

We shared a smile.

"You underestimate yourself," she said.

"You're one to talk." I gave a little snort. "And, by the way, I don't regret telling Louis what was up with you, either."

Jiggy rolled her eyes. "I love you, Camille."

"I love you, too. Whether you like it or not, you'll always be my best friend."

"Thank God." Her chin quivered. "I wasn't sure you felt that way anymore."

"I wasn't sure you wanted me to." I twisted my lips to the side. "I let you down."

"No, you didn't. I let myself down."

"Can we put it behind us?" I asked.

"Definitely. What's a fistfight or two between friends?"

We hugged, then, and didn't let go until one of the climbers screamed like a little girl as his body hurtled toward the water. Laughing, we watched them for a few moments longer, then I lay back on the blanket, folding my hands beneath my head.

"So, what's going on with Louis? I feel like we haven't talked in a hundred years."

"He's coming for a visit when we get back," she said, a ribbon of excitement in her voice.

"Cool! How long has it been? Is he bringing you back a cute gorilla?"

"Years." She smirked. "And *no*."

"That's really great. Except the no-gorilla part."

"I'm definitely looking forward to seeing him. Especially now that we've been really talking, you know? But my parents are coming back too." She gave me a meaningful stare. "Early."

"Uh-oh."

"Yeah." She reached over and plucked off a ginger blossom, twirling it beneath her nose. "The board of directors at MA launched an investigation about the Brett blog after his parents got wind of it. They read it, by the way, and freaked out."

"No!" Okay, it was sort of cool that his parents had read it! "I can't believe you haven't told me."

"We haven't exactly been chatty."

She had a point.

"So, I guess I wasn't as careful as I'd thought." Jiggy pressed her lips into a grim line. "My parents had received a couple of calls about it. When they mentioned it to Louis, he admitted I'd written it." She threw me a sidelong glance. "Told you he'd breach the whole sibling-confidentiality rule."

"It's just because he cares."

"I know." She tucked the sides of her hair behind both ears. "He even stood up for me as much as he could. So, anyway, I guess I have to come clean with the administrators at MA."

My heart clenched. "What's going to happen? Are they going to expel you?"

She shrugged. "I guess I'll find out soon enough. It's weird. I'm ambivalent about the whole thing. Maybe a little scared, but really, I just want to get it over with and move on. I can't deny I did it."

"True." I wasn't sure how to react to this news "Well, you know I have your back."

She nodded, then grinned. "Want to hear something that makes it all worthwhile, though?"

I sat up. "What?"

"I guess Brett is the laughingstock of Madison. One of my friends from Computer Club told me his house gets hit constantly with toilet paper, girls' underwear, and teddy bears."

"That is AWESOME."

"Yeah. He's not even able to laugh it off anymore, since all those other girls came forward to say he lied about having had sex with them, too. I guess he's actually still a virgin."

What a beautiful piece of justice THAT was. "And I bet he'll stay that way for at least another year, now that everyone knows his business." We shared evil grins.

"His parents made him join the youth group at their church. And they sent him to a psychotherapist."

"Man, you know all the good gossip. I know I wasn't so sure about the blog, and I'm sorry you got caught, but I owe you big-time."

Her expression softened into something just a little sad. "Actually, Cam . . . I think we're just about even."

"It's going to be okay, Jiggy." I put my arm around her shoulders and squeezed.

"I hope so. And, hey, look at the bright side: My parents have *finally* taken notice of me."

I snorted. "Wait until they see your piercings."

She rolled her eyes. "I already warned them. I was afraid the shock might do them in. I think I'm going to let the nipple piercing heal up."

"Glug!" I feigned dizziness, then laughed. "You're crazy, you know that?"

"Yep!" She raised her shoulders, then let them drop on a sigh. "And darn proud to know that I'm SO MUCH like my best friend. Now, go climb that waterfall, wingnut!"

I hate to admit weakness, but that waterfall was the most difficult climb I'd ever made. It didn't help that the rock was slightly wet. Knowing everyone was watching me, I kept my focus directly on the fixed pro. I tamped down my fear and worked my way slowly from one to the next, and so on, carefully hooking in, checking, and double-checking each time. When I finally reached the jump point, my muscles were seriously chimed, partly from the exertion, but mostly from the tension. The climb wasn't *that* technical, but it went straight up, and the deafening sound of the waterfall made it a zillion times more frightening.

I'd never been so stoked as when I'd hooked securely onto that last bomber bolt, mostly because I knew it was almost over. I let my body hang for a minute as I took a few deep breaths and stretched out my cramped hands.

Okay, I made it.

What now?

Oh yes, the jump. I remembered watching Faustino

turn toward the water before he unhooked, so that seemed like a logical next step. What I failed to recall was the dude's utter lack of fear. I made the mistake of swinging outward quickly and glancing down at the same time.

My breath left me in a whoosh. "Holy crap," I whispered, and just that quickly, I was gripped. I was freakin' WAY up high. How come it hadn't looked so far up when the other guys were hanging on the bolt? More important, how had I forgotten that I'd always been afraid of the high dive at the pool??

Seriously, I couldn't MOVE. Not even to swing back toward the wall and regain my composure enough to find a foothold with which to start the descent. Because there was NO CHANCE IN HELL I was going to jump.

But, all of a sudden, I became aware of the fact that I didn't even have enough strength left to climb down. And yet the thought of jumping paralyzed me with fear.

What if I did something wrong?

What if I flailed on the way down and struck the rocks?

What if I passed out from fear and drowned?

Exhaustion made it impossible to climb down.

Fear made it impossible to jump.

Stuck. My breathing quickened. I was SO screwed.

The whole group stood below me, so small from Way Up Here, they looked like those surf-gnomes and hula-fairies I'd wondered about earlier. All their little gnomey faces were tipped up, watching me with eager expectation.

I started laughing, and couldn't stop. I think they call it hysteria. And then, as quickly as I'd busted into laughter, I started crying. Tears sprang to my eyes, and I just let them fall. Screw it. None of the gnomes could see my face from Way the Frig' Down There on the enchanted forest floor, anyway, and I clearly needed to release some pent-up tension.

I totally had to pee.

"Camille!" Makaio called out. "Unhook and go for it!"

Yeah. Sure. When I was certain my voice wouldn't give away the full extent of my fear, I yelled out, "I can't."

"You just have to reach down and unclip," he said, going through the motion as though he thought I'd forgotten how.

"That's not it," I yelled. "I seriously can't do it."

"Sure, you can!" Faustino hollered, hands cupped around his mouth like a megaphone.

I watched Jiggy stand and shade her eyes with one bladed hand. All the gnomes mobilized, moving forward to yell out instructions or encouragement. What they failed to grasp was, nothing they said mattered. I wasn't exaggerating one little bit when I said I COULD NOT move.

I hung there until my hands started to tingle, and desperation bubbled up inside me. I started picturing things like helicopter rescues and front-page news articles. I suddenly wondered if I'd remembered to wear my swimsuit or if I was hanging there bare-assed.

Attempting this had been a massive error in judgment.

And now I totally, TOTALLY had to pee.

I let my mind wander to more familiar things, more logical topics. I needed to focus on something I could control.

The ozone in the upper layers of Earth's atmosphere is beneficial, _______ animal and plant life from dangerous ultraviolet radiation.
(a) withdrawing
(b) thwarting
(c) displacing
(d) reflecting
(e) protecting

"Protecting," I muttered. "Easy."

John realized that he had been _______ in his duties. If he had been more _______, the disaster may have been avoided.
(a) irreproachable......careful
(b) arbitrary......interested
(c) neglectful......insensible
(d) derelict......vigilant
(e) unparalleled......careful

"Um . . . um, it's . . . derelict and vigilant."

My legs launched into huge-ass death wobbles, as though they belonged to someone else's body. I closed my eyes and went very still.

Being a man of maxims, he was ________ in what he said.

(a) sentient

(b) sebaceous—

"Cam!" Makaio called.

My eyes snapped open. "Yeah?"

"What are you doing?"

I stared down at him. "Practicing SAT questions in my head," I yelled back.

In an instant, he had run over to the supplies and begun to harness up. He whipped a glance my way. "Hang on!" he hollered. "I'm coming up. Just relax."

I'd never been so happy in my life. I swallowed convulsively a few times until I knew I wouldn't sound like a panicky dork, then yelled, "Hurry up!"

chapter fourteen

"Hey," Makaio said, when he'd reached the bolt just below mine. By then, I was well into the SAT math section in my head, and the rushing sound of the waterfall had become pure white noise. Insanity had to be the next stop on this carnival freak-ride.

He smiled. "Funny meeting you here."

"Yeah, you're hilarious," I said, on a long exhale. "Now, get me down from here."

His smile evaporated as quickly as it had appeared. "Cam, I can't get you down from here. You have to jump."

My heart squeezed. "Very funny. You're a regular Jay Leno. But, seriously. Get me down."

We locked stares for several long moments.

Panic started to screech in my ears. "I mean it, Makaio. Get me down!"

"Camille, listen to me carefully," he said, in the ol' talk-a-suicidal-jumper-off-the-ledge tone of voice. "There are two ways down from this spot. Just two." He held up two fingers in a V. "You can jump, or you can climb."

"You came all the way up here just to tell me that?" I yelled. He ducked just in time to avoid getting my shoe in his head. "Okay. You win. I am afraid, just like you said all summer long. YOU WIN. Now, please, please, PLEASE get me down before I seriously freak out."

"Camille," he said, over-enunciating every word in a raised voice, "I can't get you down. There's no way. If you don't want to jump, then turn around and climb down. I'll guide you from below."

My chin started quivering. Defeat enclosed me like a body bag—zzzzzzzzzzzzip! "I can't." And then I started to cry.

"Hey, it's okay. Why can't you?" he whispered, reaching up to hold my foot. I found it oddly comforting.

"Because my muscles are fried. I honestly don't have the strength. And I hate the high dive. I've always hated the high dive. Why did you make me forget that?" I'd regressed into a sniveling, wimpy-ass, blame-making mess, and I didn't give a damn. Big, fat tears rolled down my face. I wiped them away with a sweaty, shaky hand.

"You don't have to dive," he said, all cheery. "It's just a quick, easy jump."

I sniffled. "I hate you."

"I know."

"This is all your fault."

"I know." He patted the top of my shoe.

For a few minutes, I cried and he kept up the weird shoe-comforting motions.

"Listen," he said, as if he'd just come up with a super-ingenius plan. "Just jump. Go for it. One, two, three-"

"No."

He sighed. "You're in perfect position."

"I don't care. I can't."

He gestured below us. "All of us have done this jump hundreds of times, and look. We're all fine."

I glanced down. Faustino waved. "No, you're all freakin' insane. That's no comfort."

"All you have to do is unhook. Gravity does the rest."

I scoffed. "Yeah, that makes me feel a whole lot better. Thanks. Ever considered working on a suicide hotline?"

He ignored my sarcasm like a pro. You would think he'd known me forever. "I'll jump first, and then I'll wait in the water for you, yah? I'll swim over to you right away."

I shook my head. "I'll probably land on you and kill us both."

"You won't. I know where to wait."

"You don't understand, I can't."

"I *do* understand. And, you can. It'll be over so fast," he said, snapping his fingers. "I promise."

Annoyance flashed through me, and I kicked in the vicinity of his head again. "God, Makaio! You know exactly what I've been through, thanks to Jiggy. And yet you tell me to jump. You tell me it's fine, easy. Just 'unhook—gravity does the rest,'" I mimicked. "All smiles and fun. You expect me to just blindly trust you?

Well, news flash, I'm not that trusting of a person yet, okay?"

He stared up at me for several long seconds, then his face spread into a smile. "You've got it all wrong, babe."

"What are you talking about?" I blinked. Hold up—did he just call me "babe"?

"I don't want you to jump because I tell you to," he explained. "That's crazy talk. And it doesn't matter at all whether or not you trust me, eh."

"Huh?"

"You can do this, Camille, and it has nothing whatsoever to do with me. *E hilina`i `oe iā `oe iho.*"

I spread my shaky arms wide. "Which means?"

"It means, 'trust yourself.'" And with one last thumbs-up, Makaio unclipped, plunging below me into the water.

"Damn it!"

I closed my eyes and took some deep breaths. In . . . out . . . in . . . out. Just unclip and jump. Could I do it?

Easing my eyes open, I peered below me. Way, way, wayyyyyyyyyy down. Makaio was there, treading water off to the side. He waved, then yelled, "*E hilina i `oe iā `oe iho.*"

Trust myself?

And hadn't that been one of my goals for the summer? The question was, had I reached that goal?

"Camille!"

I looked down to see Jiggy standing right on the edge of the water. "Hey!"

She curved her hands around her mouth. "I have a question for you!"

"Yeah?"

"What is the worst that could happen if you jumped?"

I blurted a laugh. "Shut up, are you crazy?"

"Answer me!"

I sighed. "Fine. I could hit the rocks and die!"

"No, you couldn't. You're in the right spot! Try again!"

"I could wet my pants on the way down!"

The gnomes laughed.

"It's okay," Faustino hollered. "You hit the water. No one will know."

Okay, the guy had a point.

"What is the worst that could happen if you jumped, Camille?" Jiggy asked again.

I thought about it. "The water could rip off my bathing suit and I'd be totally naked."

"She said the worst thing, not the best thing," Faustino yelled, in his typical teasing fashion.

I laughed. "Shut up, pervert!"

"What is the worst thing, Camille?"

"I'm afraid!"

"SO?" Jiggy said. "Answer my question."

I thought about it for a long time, and I couldn't come up with much. I mean, the peeing thing? Not a problem after all. My swimsuit was pretty stable. I wasn't going to land on the rocks and die. I wasn't going to land on Makaio. Had he really called me "babe"?

"I guess the worst thing isn't jumping," I yelled down to her. "It's actually the unclipping part!"

"Okay, then what's the worst thing that could happen if you *don't* unclip?"

I reached up and shoved the hair back from my forehead. "I guess I could just die up here."

Jiggy spread her arms wide. "That's right! So freakin' jump! If I'm brave enough to go before the Midwest Academy board of directors and admit what I did, you're brave enough to unclip!"

"How do you know?" I asked.

"*E hilinā`i `oe iā `oe iho*," Makaio yelled.

Jiggy pointed toward him. "What he said!"

I looked at Jiggy. At Makaio and Faustino. At all the gnomes who simply believed in me for no other reason than . . . they just did. And all of a sudden, I realized I could have this kind of faith in myself, too. I *did* have this kind of faith in myself. I could return to MA with my head held high. I could seriously ROCK the SAT. I could stare right at Brett, unblinking, and tell him to kiss my ass.

On second thought, I'd tell him he wasn't *worthy* to kiss my ass. Laughter bubbled up inside me, and for no real reason, I suddenly saw the truth.

I was strong enough. Smart enough.

I could do anything I set my mind to.

If nothing else, I'd proven that to myself this summer.

The misstep today had been climbing this damn waterfall.

All that remained was the correction.

A sense of calm washed over me as I knew what I had to

do. “Screw it,” I yelled. And unclipped. Then I screamed, long and loud . . . falling . . . falling . . . until the cool, blue water sucked me under.

Almost instantly, hands grasped my upper arms and pulled me to the top. I emerged breathless, gasping. Laughing. Makaio and I were under the waterfall, and he was smiling bigger than I'd ever seen him smile before.

“I knew you could do it,” he said.

I stared into his eyes, treading water, holding on to his shoulders and breathing heavy. “M-Makaio, I have to tell you something.”

“Go for it.”

I swallowed a couple of times, then licked my lips. I couldn't seem to regulate my breathing. “You're too old for me. You'll be twenty-one soon.”

He blinked. “O-kaaaay.”

“I'm only seventeen. Well, almost eighteen. B-but . . .”

His eyes sparkled. “Yeah?”

Go for it, said that small voice inside me, the one I knew I would always believe in. *Trust yourself*. “But you won't be too old for me next summer.”

And then I kissed him.

Lo and behold, he kissed me back. Right there in the water, wrapped in each other's arms, with the waterfall splashing over our heads. He tasted like sunshine and freedom. He tasted like promise.

What's the worst that could've happened if I hadn't jumped?

I could've missed out on THIS.

www.NobodyGetsJiggy.com

NEWS OF THE DAY!!!! C kicked butt on the SAT! She'll have her pick of colleges, but I just have a sneaking suspicion she'll be heading to her first choice school, Island-Pacific College, in Hawaii, after we graduate.

Um, because her GRANDMOTHER lives there now.

Uh-huh, sure. That's the reason why. Trust me!

JUST KIDDIN', C!

Actually, C's always wanted to go to a college near her grandmother, and now that Grandma has moved to Hawaii, it's just the even more PERFECT choice. Sure, it's a convenient coincidence that M attends school there, too, and that the two of them are now as inseparable as two people living thousands of miles apart can possibly be. I choose to believe that things happen for a reason in life!

Plus, it'll be WAY easy to transfer those credits we both earned for the work-study gig on the ship. Did I mention we each got a big fat A+ on our required projects?? Yeah, we rule.

Speaking of things happening for a reason, I'm one hundred hours into my four hundred hours of school-ordered community service. I almost feel guilty, because it doesn't feel like punishment at all. (And then again, I don't feel guilty, because I'm being "punished" for a community service: letting everyone know the TRUE Brett Mason. I'm sort of a cyber Robin Hood, if you will.)

Anyway, I'm teaching computer stuff to the residents at the senior living facility near our house. I swear, it's like I have hundreds of adopted grandmas and grandpas now. They nag me about what I'm wearing, where I'm going. One particular lady (who insists I call her Memaw) actually makes me CALL her when I get home from dates.

I'm in HEAVEN!

C thinks I'm nuts, but one person's heaven is another person's nightmare—what can I say?

So, I've decided to double major in computer science and geriatrics and continue working in this industry. I never knew old people could be so fun! My parents think it's a great choice too. But, before I head off to college, I have to graduate, and after I graduate, I'm going to spend one final summer with my mom and dad in Tanzania. They're sort of making me. Don't tell them, but I'm actually looking forward to reconnecting with the chimps. Some of the ones I knew from years ago are still there!

And, okay, it'll be good hanging with the parentals, too. Especially now that we've cleared the air. Things aren't PERFECT between us, but we're getting there. And Louis and I have never been closer. We e-mail every day. He may be old, but he's funny and smart and easier to talk to than I ever imagined. I finally have a BROTHER.

Summary? All's good in blog universe. AND,

believe it or not, in the real world, too. So I'll catch you on the flipside and fill you in as things progress. I mean, what's the worst that could happen?

Kisses—The Goddess

Lynda Sandoval is a former police officer turned fiction writer with fourteen adult books to her credit. Her first book for teens, *Who's Your Daddy?*, won the National Readers' Choice Award for young adult fiction from Romance Writers of America and was a finalist for the Colorado Book Award. When Lynda is procrastinating, she loves to quilt, hike, garden, make jewelry, bid obsessively on eBay, and read everything she can get her hands on. She lives in Denver with the world's coolest cairn terrier, Smidgey.